"Why didn't you tell me you were here?"

"The truth?"

She took a bite of cake and smiled indulgently. "Nothing less."

"I saw you come out here, and all I could think about was what happened yesterday. I'm talking about you and me on that balcony, Danica. What could I have said to you tonight that wouldn't make things awkward for us both?"

"What about 'Hello'?"

Dex raised his brows. Then he gave the slightest of nods and slowly moved in close. Taking full advantage of the fact that she was positively paralyzed with anticipation, he stepped behind her. His fingers tantalized her neck as one hand smoothed her hair. Cool night air touched the nape of her neck just before his warm, firm mouth did.

Lazily, he left a path of those hot, full-pressure kisses from her hairline to the carefully tied bow that held her halter gown in place.

When his hand slid off her shoulder and roamed to cover her breast, all she could do was arch into his touch with a shallow sigh. Carnal agony.

Books by Lisa Marie Perry

Harlequin Kimani Romance
Night Games
Midnight Play

LISA MARIE PERRY

thinks an imagination's a terrible thing to ignore. So is a good cappuccino. After years of college, customer service gigs and a career in caregiving, she at last gave in to buying an espresso machine and writing to her imagination's desire. Lisa Marie lives in America's heartland, and she has every intention of making the Colorado mountains her new stomping grounds. She drives a truck, enjoys indie rock, collects Medieval literature, watches too many comedies, has a not-so-secret love for lace and adores rugged men with a little bit of nerd.

MIDNIGHT *Play*

Lisa Marie Perry

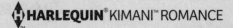

HARLEQUIN® KIMANI™ ROMANCE

For the wild one—
You changed my life for the better.
But of course you already knew that.

Recycling programs
for this product may
not exist in your area.

ISBN-13: 978-0-373-86364-8

MIDNIGHT PLAY

Copyright © 2014 by Lisa Marie Perry

For questions and comments about the quality of this book please contact us at CustomerService@Harlequin.com.

HARLEQUIN®

Printed in U.S.A.

www.Harlequin.com

Dear Reader,

I've never been known as a particularly bad seed. Or an especially good one. Just an average gal, with plenty of virtues and some vices thrown in to keep things interesting. That being said, I've always been fascinated with good seeds—people who *seem* immune to mistakes, who *appear* to make the best decisions and effortlessly live well.

Writing *Midnight Play* put me inside the head of a woman who fits this description. If you've read *Night Games,* you know that, unlike her "rule-breaker" sisters, Danica Blue is considered a "rule-maker." Yet Danica's deeply passionate relationship with badass quarterback Dex Harper reveals that she's more than who she is perceived to be. Meeting Danica's bad-girl side gave me the chance to get acquainted with Dex's good-guy side. And one hell of an adventure it was!

Welcome back to The Blue Dynasty.

XOXO

Lisa Marie Perry

Chapter 1

What a beautiful lie.

Under the dusky blush of sunset the Venetian was a spectacular beacon, polished inside and out—a true Las Vegas gem. The air was sweet with late-summer blooms. Inside, the marble floors echoed as Danica Blue marched—anyone who knew her knew she didn't simply walk or strut or glide, but instead *marched*—to her destination within the grand hotel.

The engraved invitation was to an elegant late-afternoon tea, but Danica didn't harbor a shred of doubt that a raunchy bachelorette party awaited.

At the double doors of the Renaissance suite, she paused, going over a mental checklist. The chiffon-green tea-length dress she wore was simple and strapless, designed for just this occasion—so she had no concern there. Despite the sunshiny afternoon, she'd driven to the Venetian with the top of her silver Porsche Boxster up to protect her wispy bangs and side-swept braid from the wind. With hair and makeup on point, that left her posture.

From the time Danica had been four and toddling around in her mother's high heels, trying to fill Temperance Blue's shoes even then, she'd been warned that sloppy posture ruined any look.

Danica quickly corrected herself. Chin up. Chest out. Peep toes of her strappy shoes pointed forward.

Smile, damn it. It didn't matter that she was combating the effects of neglected sleep, having lately worked almost obsessively. Her high-profile career and family rarely left her a moment's peace. Not to mention how hard it was to sleep now that she lived alone in her mountain-view mansion. Yet the place still felt cluttered and claustrophobic with cobwebby memories of what used to be.

Either get an exorcist or get away, had been her friend Veda's advice. Danica's idea of exorcising the place was throwing out the bed she'd shared with her ex, splurging on a new one and hanging a row of dream catchers above the headboard. But she'd also adopted the other half of Veda's advice, even though escaping to the administration complex at Slayers Stadium and working herself into a stupor sometimes left her irritable.

Not that anyone knew this, of course. It was Danica's secret and hers alone—that she was more tired and lonely than she let on…and tired of being lonely.

She adjusted the extravagant orchid bouquet—a thank-you token for the hostess, who was likely halfway toward bachelorette drunkenness—in the crook of her arm and used the other hand to knock.

Pastel perfection greeted her as an usher guided her into the foyer and traded a dainty pink lace "freshen up" pouch, complete with hand sanitizer and mints, for the bouquet. It joined an array of bouquets in vases of varying shapes and colors, all of which paled in comparison to the centerpieces of luscious cherry-blossom branches that topped nearly every table. The wet bar was stocked, and there were hors d'oeuvres on china dishes and champagne in crystal flutes. Bunches of balloons, miles of ribbon and string lights added to the classy festiveness—as if someone had commissioned Martha Stewart herself to transform the luxury suite.

And it was a total facade, providing cover for the heart of this shindig.

There were men here. Lots of 'em. Danica worked so closely with professional football players that she could practically sense the testosterone before the door even opened. The Las Vegas Slayers had christened her "the Ball Buster" because she fearlessly went toe-to-toe with men on a daily basis and knew what made them tick. The nickname had originated when her parents had acquired the team at the tail end of the previous season and appointed Danica as general manager. She wore the title with pride and used her law education and work experience in personnel management and public relations to manage her men with creativity and confidence. She was a fresh face in sports—a woman who posed for pictures for the paparazzi, was unflappable in press conferences and could work the media in ways no one understood. And when it came to managing her parents' franchise, she was full throttle.

Nothing was more valuable than the faith her parents invested in her. They didn't trust Danica's older sister, Charlotte, or younger sister, Martha, the way they did her. At thirty, she'd fully bloomed into their dream daughter. Danica could thank herself for that achievement. She'd learned at an early age how to read people and always knew just the right thing to say or do to be in their good graces.

The power that came with being admired and envied

could make a girl feel invincible. Women wanted to be her. Men wanted to be with her.

If only that were enough for Danica. A high-powered career, tight friendships and a loving family were wonderful blessings. She was a daughter, sister, boss, friend...but as of thirteen months ago, she was no longer a wife. Somehow being someone's *ex*-wife didn't feel like an adequate placeholder. Underneath it all she was still struggling to navigate single womanhood. Or maybe she was just restless, in need of a distraction.

A roomful of sizzling-hot male strippers probably wouldn't get the job done, but she was willing to get into the spirit of things. After all, her law-school friend Veda Smart would get married only once—she'd put off committing to her jewelry designer Prince Charming for years while she played the field, because she was neurotically meticulous and wanted to be absolutely sure he was the right guy—and now she was sure.

"Girls!" Danica called into the living room, where the guests were gossiping over drinks. "What's a gal gotta do to get an appletini around here?"

Squeals. Cheers. Then a rainbow of pastels surged forward as the women stampeded to her, with Veda leading the pack.

"Finally, finally, finally!" Veda wrapped her in a tight hug, then reared back with a grin. Over her frilly white cocktail dress she wore a tee that read Buy Me a Shot, I'm Tying the Knot. It was a little ironic since the Smarts were funding everything from the bachelorette party to the bridesmaids' gowns to the wedding reception. So technically she was buying her own shots. And just how many of those she'd already downed today was anybody's guess. "What took you so long to get here?"

"Speed limits." Danica thanked the server who appeared with an apple martini. The martini and a glass of champagne would be her limit. In an hour or so she'd drive to the stadium for a night of work.

She raised her glass high overhead. "This one's for the quirky, sweet, lionhearted bride-to-be. You inspire me."

"Really?" Veda's eyes were misty with tears.

"Really. You and Mekhi—you guys show me that love truly is patient and kind and everything that people want to believe but are afraid to. Be happy." Danica lowered the glass and drank with gusto.

Veda clapped and bounced on her toes, probably relieved that, one, Danica had actually shown up to the bachelorette party after weeks of waffling, and, two, she wasn't being a Debbie Downer. It wasn't that Danica didn't support Veda's engagement. It was that Veda had it lodged in her mind that having a divorced friend in the wedding party could project negative energy onto her marriage. Danica hadn't been particularly happy to be demoted from matron of honor to bridesmaid upon her divorce, but she understood Veda's eccentricities. Part of the reason the woman was her friend was that their differences kept their friendship in a sort of balanced-out harmony.

Danica knew that Veda, a socialite who'd found her calling in geriatric advocacy and worked at a retirement estate, was a gentle soul despite her tendency to be socially mystifying. Veda wanted her once-in-a-lifetime wedding to be a happy occasion. Who couldn't empathize with that?

"So, sistas," Danica said teasingly, resolving to pretend for a while that she wasn't the divorced oddball in the group, "where are the men?"

"What men?" Veda asked coyly as the others giggled.

"Come off it. As discreet as this tame so-called afternoon tea is, you're not fooling me. I've known you since law school, and part of your dream-wedding scenario has always been a wild bachelorette party. And since Kensie helped coordinate this, I'm sure she has something naughty up her sleeve." Danica gave Kensie, who was Veda's younger cousin and maid of honor, a knowing smile. In their circle it was still mentioned how Kensie's Hawaiian-themed high-school graduation party had been canceled once her parents had discovered that she'd sent out invitations that read Get Lei'd. "Plus, I sensed virile men the moment I came up to the suite."

"Fine," Veda said. "They're in the media room. Guess I can't pull one over on an attorney."

"They're getting ready for the next number." Kensie took her empty glass and passed it off to a server. "You missed the first one. Man, did they work it! It was *incredible*."

"Bummer." It wasn't *that* much of a loss to Danica, who had easy year-round access to Las Vegas's male revue talent like Chippendales and the Thunder From Down Under, should she ever want to indulge in that brand of entertainment. The urge had never struck her. She'd gotten married at nineteen and divorced at twenty-nine and was now too preoccupied with other obligations to get her kicks watching men "work it."

Besides, what would it do to her reputation to let people think that she frequented strip shows? What might her parents say? She couldn't quite picture their reaction because she'd never yet disappointed them.

That honor went to her sisters. At the moment it was Charlotte who was in the hot seat. Three weeks into the new season, she was still wading through sports-media infamy for having a tryst with a fellow assistant athletic trainer during the Slayers' training camp. Danica was doing all she could to smooth things over, but it wasn't easy. They were fire and ice—Charlotte a rule breaker and Danica a rule maker. And sometimes it was only by the miracle of sisterly love that they coexisted in the same family.

"Well, we'll make sure you get extraspecial attention now," Veda promised with a giddy laugh as sultry music began to sweep the room. The women scattered throughout the spacious suite, cursing between laughs as they competed for the best seats.

Danica was headed for the bar when Veda grabbed one wrist while Kensie grabbed the other, and together they tugged her toward a settee that had been placed in the center of the living room.

The music switched tempo and four tall, dark and gorgeous men emerged, all dressed in firefighter gear—probably to tickle Veda's men-in-uniform fantasies. The guys were big on audience participation, and it didn't take long for Danica to be swept into the moment. Being sandwiched between two gyrating dancers who were as muscular as WWE wrestlers was fun. She could confess that. But even as she laughed and shook her booty and slid a crisp twenty-dollar bill into one man's underwear, she kept her to-do list in mind. Contracts to review. A meeting to confirm with the counselors at Faith House, the organization she'd founded to benefit at-risk teens. An appointment with her jeweler to pick up the sapphire earrings she would give Veda as her "something blue" on her wedding day.

When the strippers' attention turned to the bride-to-be, Danica slipped into the guest powder room to cool down and update the to-do list stored on her phone.

She pressed the phone against one ear and a hand against the other in an attempt to hear a voice-mail message from her assistant, Lilith. As she listened, a furious red haze descended over her vision.

"Will you be sitting in on tomorrow's meeting with Dex

Harper? Marshall and Tem have him down for noon in the Slayers Club Lounge."

"The *nerve* of that guy!" When Danica had given the quarterback his walking papers, he'd proceeded to try to get reinstated. It wasn't going to happen. She'd told him so. Now he'd gone over her head to the people she answered to—her parents, the team's owners.

She had to make a move and reestablish her control on the Dex Harper situation, which she couldn't do from a hotel suite that overflowed with liquor and strippers in varying shades of hard-bodied nakedness.

Offended and thrown off-kilter, she tossed the phone into her handbag and left the powder room without giving the mirror a glance. The strip show was in intermission now, with hip-hop music pumping down onto the party. The guests had flocked to the bar for refreshments and were raving about the dancers. Veda was now missing the tee she'd been wearing over her dress. One of the strippers would probably be taking it as a souvenir. Danica joined Veda and poured herself a flute of champagne.

"This is fun," Veda said, but the words sounded more like a question, as if she were asking for reassurance that throwing a wild bachelorette party was worth the risk to her rep should her conservative family get wind of it.

"Very. Does your boy know you and Kensie did this?" Danica asked. At her friend's worried expression, she hastened to add, "I'm not judging you. Just asking a question."

"Mekhi says he's fine with it."

"But…?"

"It's a little unsettling, that's all. These dancers remind me that there are so many men out there—millions!—and the day after tomorrow I'm going to officially choose one. I've met only a fraction of the men in the world."

"Veda, you do realize it's not humanly possible for you

to meet every man on earth." Danica chuckled, getting a nervous giggle in return. "There's a reason you said yes to Mekhi."

"Love. I love him." Veda poured a glass of champagne but didn't drink. She only eyed the bubbles rising to the flute's brim. "But couldn't love steer a woman wrong? I don't want to waste my life on a marriage to the wrong man."

Ouch. Danica blinked but wouldn't let herself make a big deal out of her friend's prewedding jitters. "I'm pretty good at reading people, V. And I see happiness at the end of your story. Mekhi loves you. You don't need to meet every man on earth if you've already found the right one."

Veda set down her glass. "Thanks, Danica."

A burst of laughter collided with a blast of music.

"Oh, no," Veda groaned. Kensie had hooked up her tablet to the sound system. Bouncing off the walls was a familiar disco song about a destructive relationship.

Embarrassment hit Danica like a blow to the gut. It shocked her, that the song's lyrics could affect her and that a friend could find humor in her failed marriage. The sheepish expression on Kensie's face told Danica that she'd pegged her right. It was a joke, and Danica was the butt of it.

"Kensie," Veda admonished. "Change songs. Right. Now."

"Sorry, Danica," Kensie offered, obeying Veda's sharp order. "I was just goofing around—trying to get you to stop being so *serious.*"

Veda made a slicing motion across her throat to shut up her cousin. She placed a hand on Danica's arm. "I don't know what to say."

"It's cool," Danica insisted. "The world's still turnin'.

I just wonder how anyone can stand to take their clothes off to this song."

A moment later came the sharp, sexy opening notes of a Def Leppard hit.

"This is better," Danica said with a sip of champagne.

"Much." Veda paused, her head cocked in thought. "Actually, I think *I've* taken my clothes off to this song."

The guests leered, and Danica finished her drink. Time to go. It took a few minutes to convince the group that work beckoned and she wasn't going home to wallow in self-pity.

"Don't worry about me," she told Veda, hugging her goodbye in the foyer. "I'll see you tomorrow for the rehearsal dinner. In the meantime, please go easy on the drinks. You don't want to be hungover during the rehearsal. It won't look good."

"Whatever you say, Miss Perfect. Oh! Wait right there." Veda held up a finger, dashed off and returned with a pink goody bag that she promptly stuffed into Danica's oversized purse. "Party favors. Night!"

There was something mischievous about the wink her friend added as she shut the double doors, but Danica was already switching to full work mode, shoving handsome strippers out of her thoughts. There was only one man on her mind: Dex Harper.

Chapter 2

"A meeting with Dex Harper. Can you make that happen?" Danica sat in her Porsche, the top down and the balmy breeze licking her skin as she tapped the steering wheel and willed the rush-hour Vegas traffic to unclog.

She adjusted her Bluetooth as her assistant vowed to get on it right away and text message her an update. "Thank you, Lil. I want to see him in my office before he meets with the owners at noon tomorrow. He needs to know that jumping over the chain of command is something that's not done inside our organization." Marshall and Temperance Blue had given her direct orders to relieve the starting quarterback of his duties with the Las Vegas Slayers. The man had maintained a noteworthy record until two seasons prior when he'd started getting sacked and picked off, showing slipshod leadership and trashing his stats. Danica had agreed with her parents' decision to cut him from the team. So she'd signed up Brock Corday, a quarterback with commendable talent and an excellent off-field reputation.

Good thing Marshall and Tem had trusted their gut, and trusted their daughter. Just recently it had hit the NFL and the media that the former owner had bribed players to manipulate the outcome of games. Dex had claimed that he was getting screwed over in a conspiracy, but no one could prove it yet, and until they could, no team would stick their neck out for him. The man was a liability that not even the most desperate of franchises wanted to touch.

Dex was mourning the loss of his career. He couldn't seem to comprehend that his time with the Slayers was over, and he was no longer the face of the team. He was no longer Sin City's devilishly handsome quarterback with a new girlfriend every month and a rebellious attitude that excited some and annoyed others. He'd lived by his own rules—rules that didn't always coincide with the National Football League's code of conduct.

The man was trouble.

Letting him go had just been good business. Danica had been pleased that her parents approved of her pick of a replacement quarterback. Yet now apparently they'd gone ahead and agreed to meet with Dex. They had undermined her.

As soon as she got settled in her office, she would get them on the phone and find out why.

As nine o'clock approached, she finally made it to the administration complex, located southwest of the stadium. The franchise was undergoing a face-lift, which included everything from brand-new turf on the field to building renovations to personnel changes.

Danica let her body relax as she took an elevator to the ninth floor and navigated the hushed halls to the managers' wing. Her office and Lilith's shared a corridor that was vibrant with the vintage-meets-bohemian-Gothic décor that the women had agreed on the day Danica had treated Lilith to a shopping day.

As Danica had expected, Lilith had left for the night. Her door was shut and there were no signs of life coming from inside her office. Danica often worked deep into the night, like so many upper-level stragglers, and never asked her assistant to hang around for company.

What Danica *hadn't* expected was to find a man waiting in an armchair in the corridor. And for damn sure she hadn't expected that man to be Dex Harper.

Startled, Danica dropped her purse. It hit the floor with a thud, and slid across the polished surface. Even as the contents of her purse tumbled out, her eyes remained centered on Dex.

"Why are you in my office?" She was more annoyed than afraid. Besides, her parents retained a team of highly paid, highly skilled security experts who were always present, alert and knew how to make themselves invisible.

"*You* called the meeting. All I did was show up, like I told Lily I would."

Lily. He was on a nickname basis with her. It surprised Danica even when she knew it shouldn't have. Lilith Laurence was a free spirit with the kind of bedazzling personality that made strangers feel as if they were lifelong friends.

Danica spun to locate her phone and felt the skirt of her dress sway about her thighs. Then she knelt, found the phone still secure within her purse and checked the screen. There was the text from Lilith, informing her that Dex had agreed to meet with her and would be at the office in a half hour. Danica hadn't guessed that Dex would be willing to drop any evening plans to get face time with the exec who'd fired him.

She certainly hadn't been prepared for him. And when you were dealing with a man like Dex, preparation meant everything.

With an involuntary cringe she imagined how she must've looked marching into the corridor, with her hair windblown from drive. And now she was flustered and snatching random items off the floor to shove back into her purse.

Oh, boy. Dex rose from the chair, which practically sighed to be relieved of his six-five, two-hundred-twelve-pound frame. Danica had reviewed his file so many times that she knew it by heart, and she could tell by the way his body filled his dark pants and gray shirt that he was all lean muscle.

He had height and strength and control—physically he was any team's dream come true. But she suspected that he had let greed get the best of him. Though he insisted he was no longer under investigation in connection with the former franchise owner's alleged corruption, until the NFL commissioner's office made a formal announcement confirming that fact, he would be little more than eye candy.

Eye candy, all right. Dex had mussed dark hair, a light scruff over a strong jaw and those arresting Paul Newman–blue eyes with touches of gunmetal—as if he wasn't beautiful enough. In a fluid motion he lowered to his haunches. His tanned skin contrasted with her own sun-kissed brown complexion as he tried to press something into her hand.

At her hesitation, he urged, "Here. Your, uh, personal items scattered when you dropped your purse."

Danica took the tiny item, and finding it unfamiliar, twisted it to read the label. Travel-size massage oil. Cherry flavored.

A gasp almost slipped out, but she pressed her lips together and watched for his reaction. But he was diligently scooping the other runaway items—a silky blindfold, a pair of mini "sex dice," a strip of condoms—into the pink goody bag Veda had jammed into her purse.

Crap. Blunders like this didn't happen to her. What could she say to kill both the awkwardness and the electric current of tension that ping-ponged between them? "These are gifts."

Dex looked her in the eyes, handing her the bag. His fingers swept her palm, and he straightened, distancing himself. Too late. His touch, despite how brief and innocent, had sparked a sensation that penetrated her flesh and was working its way into her bloodstream.

Count on a few strippers to make her overly aware of a good-looking man.

"Your…gifts…are no business of mine." But the heat that danced in his gaze as it flicked from the pink bag to her eyes told her that maybe he'd *like* them to be his business. Dex retreated to a striped chair but didn't sit. "I'm meeting with Marshall and Temperance tomorrow. I know that *you* know, and that you don't like it."

Danica got to her feet. "So why interrupt your evening to come here?"

"To hear what you have to say. It's what I've been asking for since you cut me from the team—the chance to talk and have somebody listen."

Anyone would think he'd be all talked out by now. NFL investigators were on his ass. The feds were more interested in determining the extent of the former owner's wrongdoing than redeeming Dex's name in the league and media. The corruption had run deep, and once connected the dots showed a picture of crime so clever and so veiled that it'd gone on for two years without the public being the wiser. The revelation had caught national attention and even the slightest development in the investigations was the topic of ESPN breaking news.

It didn't help that her sister Charlotte was involved with Nate Franco, a son of the former owner. Nate had been the one to tip off the commissioner's office and had refused to be caught up in his father's criminal activities.

Dex may have said that he'd never known about Alessandro Franco's scheme, but his past on- and off-field antics had earned him a reputation as a troublemaker, and that worked against him. A popular sports-channel poll showed that only 37 percent of respondents believed he was innocent.

As difficult as it was for the world to believe that nearly an entire team could be paid off to turn on its quarterback, Dex was sticking with his story.

But according to the media, he was a flop and just looking for someone else to blame.

Danica had encountered many situations throughout law school and her years as a practicing attorney that weren't black or white, but some shade of gray. There were exceptions and extenuating circumstances to consider, and there were hard lessons to be learned—one of which was that sometimes law came down to nothing but a kick-ass argument, people skills and some good publicity.

From what Danica could tell, if Dex were ever going to rehabilitate his image, he was in need of all three.

What could he tell her today that he hadn't already told investigators? Nevertheless, he was here and ready to talk. Danica saw no reason to send him on his way—yet.

Besides, the guy had chivalrously ignored that a sex-survival kit had fallen out of her purse. For that alone he deserved a few minutes of a listening ear.

"All right." Danica moved past him to unlock her office door. She swiped a panel of light switches, illuminating the comfortable space that was always visitor-ready.

He stepped in behind her. The room suddenly felt as close and airless as an elevator. At her gesture to have a seat, he chose the chair directly in front of her desk, his assessing stare not breaking for a moment. Her power and personality didn't seem to faze him. She didn't know whether that made him reckless or sincere or both. "You be 'talk,' Dex. And I'll be 'listen.'"

Dex saw the flicker of challenge in Danica Blue's eyes. He'd looked nowhere else as he'd lowered onto a striped oval-backed chair that made him think of the movie *Beetlejuice*.

I'll be damned. This is her *space?* It was almost funny that this office, with its moon lamp shades and dark miscellaneous furnishings, belonged to the woman in front of him. She was too tempting with her messy hair, taut body, smooth brown skin and that up-to-something little smirk. Covered from breasts to calves in a sexy green dress with a black bow, she looked like a present he wanted to unwrap. God only knew whatever else she was packing in that purse of hers, but already his brain and body were in overdrive at the idea of the two of them putting all those sex gifts to use.

His pants suddenly felt too tight over his crotch, and he hunched, steering his thoughts to the fact that he was unemployed. It wasn't easy, though. She was mesmerizing. Jarring. Kind of dangerous.

Which was probably exactly what she was going for.

Here was a woman who probably got a thrill watching others squirm. Well, he wasn't here to amuse her. He stared her down until she took a step back and bumped against the edge of her desk.

Playing it off, she rested her butt on the desk and set her purse down at her feet. "Uh. I offer water to every guest. Would you like one?"

Guest? That was an odd way to put it. As if she were entertaining, playing the gracious hostess—not diving into a meeting with a man she'd fired. Then again, this was her M.O. Manage a football team, chat it up with the press, terminate and replace a roomful of employees, all while wearing a pretty smile.

Pretty wasn't the word for it. More like *disarming*.

"No, thanks." He jabbed a thumb toward the open door. "Shouldn't this conversation be private?"

"This floor is management. I don't keep secrets from the people I work closely with."

Dex let his gaze drop to her purse, specifically the bit of pink that poked from the top. Danica nudged the purse under her desk with her foot. Yeah, *that* was subtle.

What she had in that bag of tricks had nothing to do with him finding his way back into a Las Vegas Slayers uniform. Dex could feel it all slipping from him—celebrity endorsements, the fame, the glory, the essence of who he'd become. At the age of eighteen he'd had to start over, reset his existence…a boy with no past and nobody to come home to. He was a self-made man, and the only place he belonged was on the football field.

Cool under pressure, man. Dex Harper had mastered the art of projecting calmness, even as his world continued to crash and blaze around him. And when it all turned to ashes, he'd survive.

"Bold move—going over my head to get a meeting with the team owners, Dex."

"I want my life back." The sting of truth stunned him.

"You mean your job with this team," Danica said.

"My job with this team *is* my life."

"Let's be honest—" Danica swept a retractable pen off the desk and began clicking it "—about what our objectives are here."

"You want a winning team. I want to help you get what you want."

"No, no, don't do that. Don't twist the situation—it's counterproductive. Two seasons straight the Slayers didn't make it to the play-offs. Your role in that? Last season in the first eight of ten games you were sacked multiple times. Over sixteen sacks in ten games!" At his furrowed brow she continued. "Wait, did you think I fired you without watching your films? I did my homework, Dex. I *know* you. I know you're from a small town, you're involved with Habitat for Humanity and you made it to pro with unquestionable skill in this game. I know you're not a quarterback who dallies around knowing there's a blitz coming. And the interceptions? You don't throw interceptions on second and goal. At least you didn't three seasons ago."

"I thought *I* was supposed to be 'talk.'"

Danica gave a short nod but continued to press the top of the pen. *Click. Click. Click. Click.*

Was there a cadence to everything about this woman? He'd heard the rhythmic strike of her high heels on the floor before she'd found him waiting outside her office. Then there was the swish of her dress that twirled every time she turned her body. Now the soft click as she toyed with that pen.

She was hypnotic. Maybe that explained how she could wipe out half of the administration and still be deemed an American sweetheart in the eyes of the media.

"Go ahead, then, Dex. I'm giving you the floor."

"No quarterback can carry an entire team. Passing and reception? That's a two-person task. When I give my boys a play, I don't expect to go out there and be left hanging.

It was deliberate, something my team planned behind my back. And all of you fell for it." The unaffected expression on her face told him that his words weren't taking hold. "If you watched my films, you saw my accuracy, my leadership, how I perform outside the pocket. I brought my team to the Super Bowl my rookie season. I brought the Slayers my first season with the team."

"You had some incredible years. I'm not pretending you didn't."

"I'm thirty-one years old, in top physical condition. Danica, I can give you more."

She dropped the pen. It landed near her purse, and while he would ordinarily have made a move to retrieve it for her, he didn't know how his body might react to another encounter with that purse.

Interesting, though. He could emerge from an onslaught of aggressive defensive linemen with a pigskin treasure secure in his grip, but she couldn't seem to hold on to an ink pen. Was there a klutz underneath her perfect exterior?

Better question, why the hell did the possibility intrigue him?

"Place an inquiry with the league, and you'll know that I'm cooperating. I didn't know why my team turned on me or why upper management didn't step in. I didn't know what it really meant when some of the guys said 'payday' after a hard hit. I didn't ask."

"Why not?"

"You ask *why* and *why not* a lot."

"Yes-or-no questions rarely give me the info I'm fishing for." She shrugged, the overhead lights glowing over her bare shoulders, the top of her dress drawing tight across a pair of high-set breasts that his large hands could palm with ease....

Dex stood, because he couldn't sit still any longer. Restlessness was riding his blood, anxiety banding around his muscles. "The truth is, I was thinking about myself. My contract. The way I saw it, as long as I did *my* job, I'd be in the clear, and when the time came for housekeeping, the front office would take care of it. I didn't push."

Her mouth opened—probably to ask *Why not?* yet again—but she blinked those long-lashed dark eyes and said, "So, what does your family think about this?"

"I don't have family to answer to." Not anymore. But if she had been as thorough about doing her homework as she'd insinuated, then she would have known that he'd disgraced his family long before losing his father, then his mother and finally his NFL career.

"Well, I do, Dex." She crossed her arms, a gesture that seemed standoffish, but on closer inspection was... vulnerable. "My expectations for this team are in line with theirs. They haven't changed their decision. Going into that meeting tomorrow, you should know that. Ignoring my authority isn't going to get you your position back. Brock Corday is our quarterback."

Dex bent, grabbed the pen where she'd left it on the floor, set it on the desk and turned on his heel to leave. "Brock Corday isn't me."

Chapter 3

Dateless. The following morning, Danica slouched ever so slightly in her chair, drummed her fingers on the linen-draped table in the Slayers Club Lounge's private dining room and stewed. Her friend Thomas had just called to say that he was on his way to McCarran International Airport to resolve a work emergency at his candy manufacturer's flagship store in Atlanta. There was no hope that he'd return to Las Vegas in time to escort her to Veda's wedding tomorrow. There was also no hope that, in just over twenty-four hours, she'd find a suitable plan B. Thomas *was* her plan B. Her on-again, off-again relationship with Ollie Johan, a polo player she'd met months after her divorce, was now permanently off.

And there was no hope that her mother would let her do the unthinkable: show up to her best friend's wedding without a date. Tem had been so desperate to ensure that each of her daughters had a plus-one lined up that she'd strong-armed her sister, Martha, who practiced free love, to commit to a man for one night only, and had curbed her criticism when Charlotte had said straight up that her plus-one would be Nate Franco or no one at all.

All who really mattered were Veda, Mekhi, their minister and a witness or two. Try convincing Tem Blue, expert on all things fashionable and high society, of that. Danica could raise the argument that in a sea of hundreds of guests, nobody would notice or care that some man wasn't wearing her on his arm. But once her mother got it fixed in her mind that she was right about something, nothing short of a filibuster could persuade her otherwise.

Danica sighed and took a generous swallow of her mimosa. A quick scroll through her phone's contacts told her that from Ewan Abrams to Scooter Zeeman, she was critically deficient in go-to guys. After breaking things off with Ollie, she'd been able to count on Thomas for those rare "must have a date" occasions. Now she didn't even have Thomas.

At eighteen she'd accompanied her parents to a garden party where she had met a sweep-you-off-your-feet young man who she was sure would give her the perfect romance, the perfect life. A few people had attempted to intervene—her older sister, her high school friends—but in Marion Reeves she had seen her happy ending. With her parents' approval—Marion was "a solid boy with his head on straight," from a respectable family—she saw no reason to slow down and think. Within a year she'd married him. He was her first, and he had been her only for years. No backup needed. Then the communication stopped, the distance set in, and as time brought Marion distinguished good looks and music-business stardom, he became someone she didn't know. His loss of interest in their marriage hadn't been a surprise. The fact that he'd come home late one night, sat her down and confessed that he'd just left another woman's bed—*that* had been the shocker. And the end of a commitment they hadn't been ready for but had kept up for the sake of appearances. Just to show the outside world that they were a power couple.

To lie to everyone, including themselves.

Danica was relieved to be free of that life, but freedom wasn't such an easy thing to get used to. Her current predicament was proof of that. She'd relied completely on her plan B and hadn't prepared a plan C.

She would keep her mouth shut should Thomas's name come up in conversation with her parents today. There was a difference between lying and not volunteering certain information, after all.

Danica peered at her delicate white-gold watch. Any moment now Marshall and Tem would arrive for their meeting with Dex Harper. Hopefully, their thoughts would be on business—not their thirty-year-old daughter's social life. Last night, after she'd gotten home and stowed away the naughty *gifts* from Veda's bachelorette party, she'd had a lengthy phone chat with her parents about their motives for having a sit-down with Dex when they had a steady starting QB in Brock Corday. They'd touched on everything from Brock's performance during last Sunday's game—he'd thrown three touchdowns but had overthrown a critical pass late in the game, inviting an interception that could've cost the team the game had the Slayers' defense not drawn a fumble—to the rotator-cuff injury he'd sustained during training camp to his mental preparedness for tomorrow's away game. Marshall and Tem sounded confident in the young man's abilities…so it boggled Danica's mind that they would even humor Dex with a meeting hours before they needed to be on the family jet and heading out of town for the game.

As much as they both wanted to go to Veda's wedding, which had been a long time coming, the event simply had the misfortune of falling on a game day. Danica was a little—okay, a helluva lot—relieved that neither her father nor mother would be hovering at the wedding. She adored them both to pieces, but every once in a while a girl needed to take a breather.

"Another mimosa, ma'am?"

Danica cast a solemn look up at the waiter who'd arrived soundlessly at her table. "Please."

"Right away." With a dimpled grin, he walked off to take care of her drink, and she discreetly swiveled on her chair to observe him. Swag. He had it.

Hmm, I wonder how he feels about spur-of-the-moment dates? Danica didn't care that he was a waiter; she only cared that he was available and not crazy.

But her parents—particularly Tem—would care.

Another sigh. Another gulp to finish her mimosa.

At eleven forty-five, her parents strode into the private dining room. Danica stood, remembering to correct her posture, smooth away the creases in her summer dress as best she could and smile as they took turns greeting her with a kiss on the cheek.

"I really have to ask again why you're even doing this," she said once they'd settled at the table, both across from her, leaving the chair beside her vacant. The waiter had rushed off again to grant her parents' request for cognac and lunch menus. "All he's going to do is plead his case, which we've all heard dozens of times already."

"We've decided—" Tem glanced at her husband, who even while sitting seemed to dominate the entire room with his towering retired-bodybuilder's physique, natural frown and those intense dark eyes "—that burning a bridge is foolish when there's something on the other side of the bridge that you want."

"So what does Dex have that you want?"

"Names."

"Names?" Danica scrunched her face in a frown, but caught the way Tem smoothed her fingers over her own forehead as a silent reminder to always be ready for the click of a camera. "What names?"

"Men on Alessandro Franco's payroll who were getting cash on the side," Marshall explained in a baritone that was still booming despite his efforts to lower his pitch. "Bribes, bounties, blackmail—it's all the same, and we want to purge our franchise of Franco's corruption."

"The league is gathering this information, though. The investigation's ongoing, but it'll all come out—"

"We need this information soon." Tem reached over to adjust the teal pocket square in her husband's ink-black Armani suit. "Before the trade deadline."

"And Dex is willing to tell you everything he knows? Ma, Pop, I find that hard to believe. None of us was willing to hear him out before. Only Charlotte was willing to listen to him—"

"Well, your sister has a special touch when it comes to wrongdoers, doesn't she?" Anger lit her mother's beautiful features. "She and Nate Franco—"

"Why would Dex even consider doing this, when there's nothing in it for him?" Danica interrupted, steering the focus away from her sister and her lover, or "partner in scandal," as Tem had once referred to him. She didn't like the tension that still hung over their family, but oh, hell, she was glad Marshall and Tem's wrath wasn't directed at her.

"Dex is just the bridge, Danica."

"The means to an end, then?"

"It's just business. You can appreciate that."

Ah. So they were using Dex to get the information they wanted to better the team—a team that would never again include him. But he must believe there was a possibility, a hope, of him returning to the Slayers. That was the only way he'd give them what they wanted. And Marshall and Tem were savvy enough to realize where Dex's weaknesses and desperation lay: his career.

"Did either of you tell Dex that he'd get his job back in exchange for names?" she inquired softly, her gaze darting between them. Both sat imperturbable, emanating power and charisma and control. They were different yet so much alike—a perfect pair.

Danica had invested years in trying—and failing— to crack their secret recipe for an unshakeable marriage.

"That wouldn't be ethical, now, would it?" said her father.

"How Dex Harper interprets things is his choice." Tem shrugged. "We haven't made him an offer—you would've known."

Except she hadn't known about this meeting until her assistant had gotten wind of it and inadvertently tipped her off.

All of a sudden her mimosas weren't settling so well.

Before she could figure out a way to convince them to cancel the meeting and trust the league to wade through the intricacies of Alessandro Franco's corporate deception, which included passing out cash bonuses to his men to tackle with the intent to injure in addition to bribing players, betting on his own team's games and even covering his tracks by falsely accusing Marshall of threatening him into selling the franchise, she saw the hostess enter the dining area with Dex close behind her.

Danica watched her parents stand to shake his hand, but

she couldn't get her own body to budge. *You're not going to like what they have in mind, Dex Harper.*

Why couldn't the man put this much effort into snagging a gig on another team? During this past spring's NFL draft, there had been several quarterback-hungry ball clubs. Even if no one picked him up as a starter, he could still be offered a backup position. He didn't have to step into yet another raw deal.

Dex paused at the chair beside her, his height and that piercing gaze tugging her full attention as he held out his hand.

Handshakes were perfectly professional. She'd look like a rude ass to ignore him. So she slipped her hand into his, and was just a bit too in tune with his strong grip, the warmth of his palm, the way his thumb caressed her skin.

He sat beside her, his gaze boldly stroking her. Quietly, teasingly, he commented, "Like that color, don't you?"

"Oh." Danica studied her emerald dress. Hold up…he'd noticed that she was wearing green again and was actually asking her what she liked? Observant. Flirted as naturally as he breathed.

"Dex," Marshall said, after taking the liberty of ordering the other man a beer, "Tem and I are aware that you're contributing to the NFL's investigation. Let's start with that."

And start they did, demanding answers that Danica knew Dex wasn't obligated to share. Sitting beside him, she felt like his counsel, and almost felt compelled to lean and whisper in his ear that he had the right to remain silent because her parents would offer him nothing—not the restoration of his job, nor his reputation. Nada.

Dex finally held up a hand, stopping the inquisition before Danica did something ridiculous like forget that she was Marshall and Tem's daughter and the team's GM. She was a spectator in this conversation. Her purpose was to sit, shut her mouth and learn.

"A lot of talking going on here," Dex said, "but none of it has to do with me. You're asking me about Franco and the coaching staff and other players. You're asking me for a list of names when you told me that we were going to talk about my file, Marshall."

"Alessandro Franco made a mess of the Slayers. That damage can't be undone, but all this right here—" Marshall outstretched an arm, indicating not just the Slayers Club Lounge, but the stadium in its entirety "—is an extension of me. I don't dig failure. Not for myself or my family, and not for my team. Any man who's so focused on a contract that he can't see the wrong that's right in front of him doesn't need to be on my payroll."

Danica felt the blow as if it had been delivered to her. She didn't know where to look, so she pretended to study the condensation on her glass as she watched Dex out of the corner of her eye.

Dex nodded, chuckling even though there was nothing funny about his circumstances. "Doing a little cleanup on the team, right, Marshall and Tem? In a hurry, too, with not too many weeks left to trade. Want me to help you figure out who to cut?" He stood. "I'm not on your payroll, so don't ask me to do a job for you."

Danica finally lifted her gaze, saw him pluck a few bills from his wallet to pay for his beer and then walk away.

"Damn it, we were so close to getting what we needed," Tem whispered.

"We still are." Marshall reached over to squeeze her shoulder. "As long as no other franchise wants him, he's still open to negotiation."

"It might be best to let him turn his attention to his own problems," Danica said, but they continued on as if they hadn't heard her. As general manager she was in theory supposed to be more of an equal, but it always seemed that she was being used more as an enforcer—just the gal to carry out their orders. It didn't matter how she got it done, so long as it got done.

"Ma, Pop, I need to step out for a moment." She was already abandoning her chair and marching out of the room. Perhaps Dex was already in an elevator, or even somewhere in the parking lot, and she had no chance of catching him. But she had to try.

She found him snaking his way toward the exit, and, picking up the pace as best as she could manage in stilettos, Danica approached and tapped him on the arm. "I thought you'd be gone by now."

"Stopped to say hello to someone I know. Is that a problem?"

"No, of course not." She cleared her throat. "A word?"

"Did your parents send you as a last-ditch effort to get answers out of me?"

"No." Danica led the way to the balcony.

It was vacant, but the rising temperature and high humidity were double trouble. The midday Las Vegas heat wrapped itself around her in an almost suffocating embrace.

And when Dex joined her, the heat worked its way completely through her.

Whatever this is you're feeling, turn it off! Time to be a professional here—a GM. Not a woman who can be unraveled by a man's criminally hot body.

"The owners have no intention of bringing you on as quarterback, Dex. I'm being frank with you—something that should've been done prior to this chat we all just had."

"Chat?" He lifted an eyebrow. "You weren't much of a part of it."

"Well, it was a meeting you'd gone over my head to set up with them, so what could I have really said? And you and I had our talk last night."

"If you remember what we talked about last night, then you know how important my career is to me. I want my life back, Danica. I want it all back."

"In the real world people don't get everything they want."

The incredulous look he sent her screamed, *What the hell would* you *know about what happens in the "real world"?* She supposed she couldn't fault him too much for assuming her life was problem free. She worked her butt off to get people to assume just that. Take her divorce, for instance. No one but immediate family and close friends knew that she and Marion hadn't amicably dissolved their marriage, that the truth was that he'd shattered her heart.

"Danica…" Good God, how did her name sound so sexy rolling off this man's tongue? "I don't think your world and mine are the same."

"Fine. Then just know that I don't want to have this conversation again. It stops here—today. The whole going over the GM's head to try to negotiate your job back? No more of that. We've moved on. It's time you did, too."

"Except no other team is interested. I'm not—how'd my agent put it?—desirable." He let his gaze sweep her mouth before capturing her eyes, her attention, her sanity. She wet her lips with the tip of her tongue, felt her nipples tighten. When his gaze touched her there, her mind became crowded with thoughts of naked bodies and hard, raw pleasure. Was it even possible for a look to throw a woman into total arousal?

Yes.

He was taking her with his eyes, and she wasn't about to tell him to stop.

Just like that, he released her by taking a step back. With a sardonic smile, he wrenched open the glass door and went inside.

Danica stared at her reflection in the glass as the door gently swung closed. Parted lips, fast breathing, pebbled nipples… She was turned on, and he knew it. "Oh, buddy. You're a lot more desirable than you realize."

Chapter 4

"I've never seen that much tongue in a wedding kiss."

Danica nudged the maid of honor in reprimand, hiding her laugh behind her pale-rose-and-ostrich-feather bridesmaid bouquet. It seemed no one else had caught wind of Kensie's comment—not the minister, who was flushed at the *enthusiasm* of Mekhi Corrine and Veda Smart's full-contact embrace, and certainly not the masses of guests and VIP media that were mesmerized at the glamour and spectacle of the most extravagant wedding Las Vegas had hosted this year. Applause, punctuated with catcalls, rang throughout Mandarin Oriental's foyer and ballroom. Women discreetly dabbed their eyes. Children squirmed and fussed, and one very distinctly whined, "Eew! Cooties!"

As for Danica, she *really* wanted cake. A nice fat slice of the six-tiered masterpiece of gourmet delight she knew was waiting to be wheeled into the ballroom. She'd eaten fruit all day to save her appetite for the decadent French-vanilla cake she had helped Veda customize with the pastry chef. And after a morning spent holed up in the bridal dressing room, filling in for Kensie, who had been shirking her maid-of-honor duties from the moment she'd arrived at the hotel late, and an afternoon spent playing nursemaid to one flower girl who'd thrown a tantrum and the other who'd gotten sick from a tummy full of rose petals, Danica thought she deserved the indulgence.

Cheers, and the beginning strains of "Por Ti Volare," escorted the couple down the petal-littered aisle, followed by the best man and maid of honor. Then the ring bearer and flower girls scampered away, and finally the groomsmen and bridesmaids paired off.

Danica's escort, a Wall Street bigwig friend of Mekhi, was too charming for words and the closest she'd come to a date for the all-day event. Unfortunately, he was also married, and after the outdoor photo shoot he'd be much too preoccupied with his wife and seven children for Danica to pretend that she wasn't the only one in the wedding party without a date.

For hours now, she'd been dodging "Who's your date?" questions and ignoring curious glances, but she hadn't been able to escape Veda's mother, the founder of Dating Done Smart, the largest matchmaking business on the West Coast. Now that Willa Smart had successfully married off her only daughter, it was her first order of business to see her daughter's best friend happily hitched. With Temperance Blue already working overtime to make sure Danica didn't stay on the shelf too long, it was going to be pretty damn tiresome to fend off two matchmaking mamas and their lists of eligible bachelors.

Danica was more interested in managing her boys. As she stood outside, letting a makeup artist dust bronzer over her cheekbones, and a seamstress's assistant adjust the lace halter bodice of her graphite Lazaro gown, she scanned the closed-off hotel grounds where the photographers were setting up and where three of the groomsmen stood engrossed in something on their smartphones. She would bet the dainty high heels pinching her feet that a football game was on each and every one of those screens.

Because she couldn't bring herself to hide her phone under her dress, and had begged her younger sister to hang on to her purse until the reception, she was without an immediate way to monitor the gridiron matchup that was happening in Texas right about now. Since becoming GM, she'd maintained perfect game-day attendance, and being disconnected from the Slayers now made her feel uncomfortable. So she sweetly thanked the makeup artist and the seamstress and hustled booty across to the groomsmen.

"Any of you fellas watching the Slayers?" she asked.

Two of the men held up their phones, showing off NFL Mobile apps. The third shrugged his broad shoulders. "Missed *American Horror Story.*"

"No judgment here." She sidled close and took one of the proffered phones. "Just want to check up on my men."

"Aren't you supposed to be gossiping and gettin' all pretty with the other honeys?"

She gave him a saucy smirk, then focused on the phone, noting the Slayers were behind a touchdown and Brock Corday was gearing up for a second-and-goal. Her brow wrinkled in concentration as she mentally urged, *Connect, damn it! Don't run the ball! Don't you dare throw an interception!* "There's no downtime for the general manager. I have to always know what's going on."

A defensive lineman made contact with Brock, gripping his waist and dragging the man backward a few paces. But Brock released the ball and it soared like a spiraling arrow toward the end zone…and into the grasp of a Slayers wide receiver.

Danica whooped in triumph, even as she watched referees assemble to review the initial touchdown call. A total delay of game, but she couldn't knock thorough officiating.

Heads whipped around, eyes stared, conversations paused at her outburst.

She composed herself as she returned the phone. "Besides, don't you think I'm pretty already?"

The trio of men grunted low chuckles at this, taken off guard by the bold question. Coming at a man—any man—from a different direction always kept things interesting. Men were more complex and unpredictable than some women gave them credit for. Danica herself had discovered that. She never would've guessed that her ex-husband, the man she'd given her virginity and fidelity to, had been getting some on the side for months before he'd decided to clue her in. And now, in reaction to just one question, three committed men showered her with laughs and *very* appreciative once-overs as she strutted away to join the other "honeys."

Veda now stood among the women, a vision in white lace and tulle, with a rather full flute of champagne. "What were you and the guys chatting about over there?"

Danica borrowed the glass and took a refreshing gulp. "Football," she answered, handing the drink back to her friend.

"Oh, work, work, work. You'll never change."

"No, why should I? Everything around me is changing plenty."

Concern drifted over Veda's face like a veil. But a photographer interrupted her response with "Picture time, ladies and gents! Follow me."

Danica was glad to be set free roughly an hour later.

She would reclaim her purse from her sister, fade into the background of the reception and eat cake.

Were there now even more guests present? Danica could scarcely squeeze past the bodies filling the Mandarin Oriental ballroom. Though plenty occupied the tea-light-and-flower-petal-accented tables, even more stood engulfed in conversation while others danced to a Lionel Richie ballad. A tuxedo here, an evening gown there. A child stepped on the hem of her dress. A security hulk bumped her, practically crushing her bridesmaid bouquet. A camera clicked, and behind it was one of the photographers Veda had commissioned to take candid shots throughout the day for her wedding album. None of the people she encountered was the one she was searching for.

Martha, where the devil are you?

Danica changed course, moving with purpose, only in passing noting the impressive floor-to-ceiling windows and the glass bubbles dangling overhead that spun the light so beautifully over the ballroom.

In the hushed, fresh-scented hall leading to the powder room, Danica froze.

Swaying slowly, in the arms of her lover, was her sister Charlotte. The sultry country love song overhead was barely audible from the ballroom, but it wasn't likely that Charlotte or Nate Franco even noticed. They were fitted together so closely, her arms draped over his shoulders and his hands curving over her hips.

A simple embrace. But the obvious passion and trust between them wasn't simple. They'd both risked so much to share moments like this. Danica knew—she was still helping to soften the consequences of their against-the-rules affair during training camp in Mount Charleston. Her sister's social life wouldn't be a juicy topic in sports media had she not struck up a relationship with Nate—had she concentrated on her job and *only* her job. But then she wouldn't have in her life a man she cared about, and who clearly cared about her. Who could observe them now, so lost in each other that they'd probably forgotten anyone else existed in the world, and not feel Charlotte had made the right choice?

Not that it was fair that Charlotte could throw out the rule book and wind up with a man who was sexy, smart and proving hell-bent on sticking with her no matter what, while Danica had followed the good girl's guide to love and marriage but would have no man in her bed tonight.

Danica feigned a cough, but instead of jumping away like a guilty teen, Charlotte simply let Nate go and turned so that she remained in his arms with his front to her back.

"I'm looking for Martha. Have either of you seen her?"

"Not since the ceremony," Nate answered, and Charlotte added, "She was talking about getting a hold of some wedding cake."

"The cake hasn't made its grand entrance yet, and I didn't see her in the ballroom." Danica looked pointedly at the pair. "Charlotte, let's go freshen up our lipstick."

Never mind that Danica didn't have a purse—hence, no lipstick. The meaning behind the suggestion should've been clear enough: *Lose the hot guy. I need to talk to you now.*

Charlotte finally stepped out of Nate's arms, but not before twisting around and kissing him in a way that made freshening up her lipstick a very necessary task. Danica stepped into the ladies' room ahead of her sister and swept her gaze across the bank of stalls to find them all empty. "If our too-cute-for-her-own-good little sis isn't in the ballroom or the potty, there's a strong likelihood that she's in the parking lot with a different guy than the one she brought to the wedding."

"Tell me how you *really* feel," Charlotte muttered, going to the mirror to smooth her pink silk party dress. She retrieved a tube of lipstick from her bag. "There're too damn many cameras flashing around this place for even Martha to forsake common sense. Did you try her cell?"

"No phone. It's in my purse. Martha has my purse."

"Oh. *Now* your mood makes sense."

"My mood?"

Satisfied with her makeup, Charlotte offered the lipstick, then dropped it into her evening bag when Danica made no move to accept it. "You're giving off a vibe that sort of says, 'Don't screw with me.' It makes sense that you're missing your phone and you probably want to know what's going on with the team. Believe me, I get it. I was staring at my phone searching for injury updates like a madwoman until Nate took me out to the hall for a dance—" She suddenly stopped.

Danica stifled a frustrated sigh. "Why do you feel that you need to walk on eggshells around me, Charlotte? Talk to me. I'm your sister."

"And the general manager. My boss. Not too recently you reminded me of that fact."

Of course Charlotte and Martha wouldn't understand what it was to be expected to juggle managing an NFL franchise and nurturing relationships. Both "professional" and "personal" competed for the first spot on her priority list. When Charlotte's indiscretions had started to put strain on the Slayers, Danica had had no choice but to step in and pull rank. She'd do so again in a heartbeat.

Which Charlotte knew. Which was why she could no longer speak to Danica freely the way she had before their parents had acquired the Las Vegas Slayers and put their entire family in the spotlight by hiring Martha as a publicist, Charlotte as an athletic trainer and Danica as the

GM. They were young women in a men's game, and Charlotte's off-field romp with a colleague had lit the media like a match to flame. Even after Nate's resignation and Charlotte's preseason suspension, the backlash still blazed.

"Am I not helping you and Nate flip this in your favor?" After ordering a few cleverly worded interviews and press releases, the tide was subtly beginning to turn. Accomplishing that hadn't been as challenging as she'd originally imagined it would be. Part of her was sorry that her true abilities had yet to be tested. The rest of her despised the idea of gossip attached to the Blue name. It was a blemish her family didn't need when her parents were cultivating a legacy for their daughters to carry on with pride. A sex scandal in football was *not* something to be proud of. "You're not doubting my ability to communicate with the media, are you?"

Charlotte shook her head. "I'm not doubting you, Danica. You always seem to get what you want. It's just annoying that commentators and reporters and analysts and paparazzi haven't moved on from the fact that two single, consenting adults had sex."

"Because what they don't yet realize is that you two are in love. Trust me—they'll realize it soon enough. See, they don't like to admit it, but sports guys dig a love story. Love is something to celebrate, but because of your circumstances you and Nate had to keep it secret. You're star-crossed lovers."

"Is that what you're telling folks?"

"It's what they'll realize naturally."

"With your encouragement, of course."

"Of course." Danica fiddled with her bouquet, which was a little beaten but still beautiful. She brought it close to her nose, and the ostrich feathers tickled her chin. "I don't always get what I want, though, Lottie. I wanted a husband who wouldn't go around banging other women, and I didn't get that."

Charlotte took the bouquet and enfolded Danica in a hug. As the eldest sister, she was now pulling rank and reminding her that sometimes she knew what was best for Danica. Over a decade ago she'd tried to warn against a hasty marriage to Marion Reeves. On the morning after Marion had moved out of the mansion, Charlotte had come over at dawn and invited her out for a run—and it had done her a world of good. Now she was giving her a huge sister hug in a ladies' powder room because she knew Danica needed it. "Sorry, sis."

The door flew open and spurts of drunken laughter preceded two young women. One was stumbling with her ebony corkscrews bouncing over her face and her frilly dress fanning out as she spun around in an effort to figure out where she was. The other was Martha, who *looked* reasonably put together in her chic flapper-inspired outfit and finger-wave hairstyle, but was loopy from the whatever was in the conspicuous bottle she held protectively to her chest along with her purse and Danica's.

"This is Leigh," Martha said as her friend leaned on her for support. "She's in love!"

Danica lifted a handful of curls away from the woman's face. "Leigh Bridges? Her father's a CNN correspondent—a friend of Veda's family."

"But I'm in love," Leigh insisted, though no one had disputed the announcement. She perched on the countertop and rested her head against the mirror. Dazedly she said, "Don't you know what it's like? It's the best feeling there is. When you fall asleep, you can still hear his voice. And all he has to do is touch you—just once—and the sensation stays with you all night."

"I want to know what that's like," Martha whispered,

all of a sudden serious beneath the haze of inebriation. She joined her new friend on the countertop and began swinging her long legs as if she were a child and not twenty-two years old. "What if I never have what you and Nate have, Charlotte? What if I never have what you and Marion were s'posed to have, Danica?"

Thank you, Martha, and you, too, Jim Beam. Danica extracted the bottle from her sister's grasp and poured the remaining bourbon down the drain. "Boozing it up isn't going to help you get it, Martha."

"Promise y'all won't tell Ma and Pop. Please? I just want some fun, without them breathing down my neck." Martha frowned defiantly…then promptly tipped sideways and retched into the nearest sink.

In spite of watching her younger sister get sick on Jim Beam, and working with Charlotte to discreetly secure two hotel suites for Martha and Leigh to sober up in, Danica *still* wanted her cake. She politely stopped to exchange air kisses with a *People* photojournalist who was bubbling over about having VIP privileges at Las Vegas's most darling socialite's fairy-tale wedding. After cleverly avoiding a probing question about her past with polo player Ollie Johan, Danica posed for a picture and kept moving. She made it back to the reception in time for dinner, a round of toasts and—finally!—the unveiling of the wedding cake. When she was in possession of a delicate china plate made heavy with a generous slab of French-vanilla cake, she escaped outdoors to the spacious terrace to check her phone and eat in solitude.

The game had already concluded, and her parents, the head coach and the head trainer had emailed her detailed reports. At least she had something to look forward to reading when she went home tonight.

The text message from her mother begged a response, but how to answer ARE YOU GIRLS HAVING A GOOD TIME AT THE WEDDING?

Without lying outright…?

She couldn't dish the truth. *Charlotte and her beau can't keep their hands off each other, Martha's drunk and I can't seem to stop feeling sorry for myself. And, by the way, I didn't bring a date.*

Aiming for nonchalance and brevity, she sent a reply. IT'S A BEAUTIFUL NIGHT. CALL YOU TOMORROW.

A beautiful night it was. The darkness was bedazzled with city lights. A calm, warm breeze stroked Danica's straight hair as she moseyed to the retaining wall and prepared to attack the cake.

Footsteps interrupted her, and she turned around as her best friend stepped onto the terrace.

"Hey, V."

"Hey." Veda ambled over. "Can you believe I'm married?"

Danica nodded. "I knew love would find you. So, is the DJ going to play 'At Last,' or what?"

"Too cliché." They laughed, and then Veda added, "I shouldn't've switched you and Kensie the way I did. That's my girl, but she's a shitty maid of honor. She's more interested in the dinner than helping me."

Danica peered through the glass but didn't see Kensie. "Well, I should confess I've been thinking about this cake since you said 'I do.'"

"Thanks for keepin' it real." Veda's smile was pensive. "This—happiness, a good marriage—is going to happen for you, Danica. You're out here eating cake alone, but you don't have a loner's spirit. Someone's meant for you."

"No pep talk. This is *your* day. Get back in there and

enjoy it. Go. I'll be in as soon as I'm done pigging out away from all those damn cameras."

"Okay, okay. But hurry. I'm going to toss the bouquet soon."

Danica watched her friend slip back inside. Yes, she was on a terrace eating cake alone, and she wasn't ashamed in the least. As long as she was getting comfortable, she might as well give her feet a few minutes' relief from the god-awful shoes.

Balancing the plate, her purse and bridesmaid bouquet, she had no free hands. So she lifted a leg and tried to shake her foot free of the skinny high heel. No luck. She bent and positioned one foot behind the other to give the shoe a nudge—

And pitched forward.

Her plate slipped from her grasp, but her panicked "Oh, crap!" hung in the air as a man caught the dish in one hand and wound a muscled arm around her waist. She was aware of being crushed against a hard male body, of cologne with hints of rum and spice, yet her eyes were on her plate.

"You rescued my cake! I could kiss you."

She felt her heart tattoo inside her chest as she looked up into Dex Harper's eyes. He handed her the plate and whispered, "What's stopping you?"

Chapter 5

Danica should have walked away—except she had an arsenal of smart-ass comebacks ready for this guy, who had the audacity to lurk on the terrace reserved for *her friend's* wedding. Well, it *was* nice that he'd caught her in the nick of time. But he was still holding her, his arm an iron vise around her waist.

And he was watching her as if expecting an actual answer. What was stopping her from kissing him? Certainly not distance. All he had to do was lower his mouth to fit effortlessly over hers.

Lips to lips…then she'd sample his taste with a soft stroke of her tongue…then she'd open her mouth under his…

Danica squeezed her eyes shut as it dawned that she'd been staring at his mouth.

"You can put me down now, Sir Galahad."

Dex set her on her feet. "And here I was, hoping you'd make good on that offer."

"Not gonna happen. I said I *could* kiss you. Not that I *would*. Besides, it's only an expression." Danica was desperate to focus on anything but him. What was it about formal-wear that highlighted nearly every attractive detail of a man's looks, anyway? The well-cut suit seemed to emphasize his height. The titanium-colored silk necktie complemented the gunmetal flecks in his blue eyes, which were even darker now than when she'd last seen him on the balcony of Slayers Club Lounge yesterday.

Hmm. Every time she ended up alone with this man, she was left with heart-thudding horniness that she didn't know how to handle.

"So, Dex—" she maneuvered her purse and bouquet under one arm and dug into the cake "—does the bride or groom know you're hanging around in the shadows like a creeper?"

"If you're asking whether I'm a crasher, the answer's no. My date models jewelry. She knows Mekhi Corrine." He had the balls to smirk. Oh, it burned her up when men smirked at her, as if she existed for their amusement. "Another thing. Coming out here to make a call is no more creepy than hiding in the dark so no one sees you eating."

A snapshot of her shoveling cake into her mouth wouldn't appear flattering splashed all over TMZ. Not that she was obligated to explain that to him. He probably wouldn't understand if she tried to explain why she had to hide to eat cake. He dated models and actresses—women who were paid to be perfect.

"Why didn't you tell me you were here?"

"The truth?"

She took a bite of cake and smiled indulgently. "Nothing less."

"I saw you come out here, and all I could think about was what happened yesterday. I'm talking about you and me on that balcony, Danica. What could I have said to you tonight that wouldn't make things awkward for us both?"

"What about *hello?*"

Dex raised his eyebrows. Then he gave the slightest of nods and slowly moved in close while she sucked frosting from her fork. Taking full advantage of the fact that she was positively paralyzed with anticipation, he stepped behind her. His fingers tantalized her skin as he gathered her hair in his fist and cupped her shoulder. Cool night air touched the nape of her neck just before his warm, firm mouth did.

Lazily, he left a path of those hot, full-pressure kisses from her hairline to the carefully tied bow that held her halter gown in place.

When his hand slid off her shoulder and roamed to cover her breast, all she could do was arch into his touch with a shallow sigh. Carnal agony. What else could describe a need so immediate and so intense? She was wet for him— he had to know it. He had to know that the scrape of his fingertips across her hardened nipple had her desperate to have all of him.

"Hello, Danica," he murmured.

The words, all dressed up in the coarse timbre of his voice, rattled her every erogenous zone. She plucked the fork from her mouth and licked her lips to double-check that she hadn't just swallowed her tongue.

He took a step back. "By the time I'd made up my mind to just go back inside, you and the bride were already talking," he said, picking up the conversation as if she wasn't standing there nearly shaking with arousal—and furious because she was so turned on. "On the upside, I did get to play your Sir Galahad. Sounds to me like you could use one."

Danica frowned. "I don't need a hero, Dex. What I *do* need is a drink to go with my dessert."

With nothing more to say, she slipped past him and into the ballroom.

If Dex wanted to screw himself out of any chance to return to the Las Vegas Slayers roster, then kissing Danica Blue again would definitely be the way to go. But hell, yeah, he was tempted.

The temptation had begun the day she'd called him into a meeting with his agent and a few corporate higher-ups, introduced herself as the new GM and then fired him. Beyond the instant anger, in the recesses of his male instincts, was heady attraction and reckless curiosity. What would a woman like that—fragile-looking but as lethal as a poisoned dagger—be like in his bed?

Now he was aching to know. Each time he encountered her, his resistance buckled and common sense crumbled. Catching her as she'd tripped had been an automatic reaction, but what he'd gained from the contact was that for all her bravado, she was delicate to hold…a shockingly gentle weight for a man to have against his body. And damn, the way her eyes glittered like dark jewels and her lush mouth teased that damn fork as he advanced on her…

Was it a tactic? Few things were more dangerous than a woman who knew how to use her assets as artillery. Dex had watched her in televised press conferences. He'd witnessed her charm aggressive journalists into drooling stooges with just the right words, just the right expression. Was she working him the same way?

Or had the vulnerability that rose off her been real?

Dex wasn't going to take the risk. His career, his dreams

of Super Bowl victories and Hall of Fame glory, were riding on his next steps. Tonight, instead of escorting an ex to a Vegas wedding, he should've been playing on a football field in Texas. He'd placed too much trust in his boys, in the franchise's decision-makers. He regretted that now, but beyond regret, he'd learned in the grittiest way possible to be smarter.

To look out for himself—because no one else would.

Inside, Dex found his way to the bar where his date, Samantha Weatherby, was swaying to an R&B song and tossing back a drink.

"Is that a beer?"

"Yes, it is. They're all out of Jim Beam." Samantha signaled the bartender to refill her glass with a bottle of Heineken. "Our barkeep here carded me. Imagine that."

Smart man. One of her modeling selling points was that she was a chameleon and could easily be made to appear older or younger, sexed up or pure. Tonight she'd turned the dial to wholesome and could pass for any high-school boy's girl-next-door fantasy. With pale skin, big violet eyes and shiny strawberry-blond hair that was decorated with a pink streak, Samantha was for damn sure the kind of girl Dex would've loved to have had next door. Instead, his closest neighbor had been an elderly farmer with anemic cows.

Samantha was as honest as any woman he'd ever been involved with, but she had her own set of vices—like a smoking habit and anxiety and a fear of exclusive relationships. An angel with a crooked halo.

She ducked under his arm to hug him. "Did I ever tell you that you're awesome, Dexter Harper?"

"What do you want?"

She glared at him for a moment. Her lips, painted a glossy nude shade, puckered into a pout. "Cynic. I was only going to say that I really appreciate you coming with me to Mekhi's wedding. Most ex-boyfriends would've said no."

"I did say no. The first time you asked."

"But the second time you said yes."

Dex lowered his voice an octave as a chain of giggling women shuffled past them toward the dance floor. "We were both naked at the time, Samantha. I would've said yes to almost anything."

"Anyway—" she unwrapped her arms and took a sip of the beer "—I was saying that I'm thankful for you. And I met someone…here at the reception, I mean. I'm going to be leaving with him. Of course you can take off, if you want. But I wish you'd stay awhile and get the most out of tonight."

Shyness wasn't something he associated with her. No, it wasn't shyness he detected. It was guilt. "When we broke up, we gave up the right to each other's business, didn't we, Samantha?"

At least, that had been the plan. He'd dated women after her, and even though over the past several months she reappeared in his life for sexual pit stops on her way to other relationships, and tabloids couldn't grasp that sometimes a woman showed up at a man's house at two in the morning for a quick fix and not to restart a relationship, they'd lost the layer of closeness that came with being a bona fide couple.

"I care what happens to you." Samantha sipped from her glass. "Dragging you here, then leaving with some other guy…not my finest behavior."

"Would it make you feel better to know I wasn't expecting to get any from you tonight?" She jabbed his side with her knuckle, and he grinned.

"Oh, Dex. I'm trying to be serious. Don't tell me you're taking up with yet another overeager, fawn-all-over-you-type groupie. It's time you met somebody who'll treat you right. Let's see…" Samantha scanned the ballroom. "What about her? She's awfully pretty and seems capable of holding a decent conversation."

Dex watched as an Asian woman in a flowing dress held a group in rapt amusement. His gaze drifted to the hand she was waving animatedly in the air. Big-ass diamond on her finger. "She's married, Samantha. Contrary to what the general public thinks, I'm not *that* much of a bastard."

"You're not a bastard at all." Undeterred, she continued to twist left, then right, tactfully pointing out women who had the potential to be what his best friend, Russo, a defensive tackle who'd been traded from Las Vegas to San Francisco, called "one-hit wonders."

"Drop it, Samantha—"

"Oh, mister, mister," she interrupted in an excited whisper. "What about that woman? No wedding ring. She's dancing alone. Gutsy." She put her arm around him again. "Don't you see her? The one in the bridesmaid gown with her hair down."

Dex saw her, all right. A knockout from the front, Danica was just as tempting from the back. Fine-boned with a nicely shaped ass.

"Swear you'll talk to her. Dex, seriously. I want that for you."

Danica's hips rocked in time to the music. With a sexy little wiggle, she made room for a middle-aged couple on the dance floor while a scattering of men ogled her. She glanced over her shoulder and saw him. In acknowledgment, he gave a slow nod and lifted one corner of his mouth. And Danica, on display for hundreds of others, was her perfect, unapproachable self again. Not the woman who ate cake with uninhibited pleasure, who stumbled over her own feet, who carried girlish pink bags filled with sex gifts.

As guests crisscrossed the distance between Dex and Danica, he turned to give his ex a firm head shake. "No."

"Why the holy hell not?"

"That woman is Danica Blue. She dropped me from the Slayers."

Samantha's pert nose scrunched. "Oh. Well, that won't work."

No freakin' kidding. Dex reached, claimed her beer and finished it off. Though Samantha gave him a withering look, she didn't say more until a few moments later when someone announced the tossing of the garter belt and bouquet.

Despite the fact that Samantha claimed she would never be the marrying type, she made a run for the press of partygoers.

Dex hung back, sticking to the ballroom's shadows. Cameras flashed, earsplitting laughter and applause ricocheted off the walls. A lacy garter belt flew into a crowd of rowdy men. Then women and girls of varying ages formed an eager cluster in the center of the dance floor.

Again, Dex was able to spot Danica. Forgetting about her would be best for his sanity, but his brain wasn't in control right now. Other, more demanding, parts of his anatomy had taken over. He crossed his arms and ventured forward, his footsteps sure and strong but soundless under the heart-pumping hip-hop music.

The bride flung her bouquet behind her, and a sea of hands shot up. It flipped a few times as it descended onto the crowd.

Dex watched Danica—subtly yet deliberately—shift to the left. And the bouquet dropped into the frantic grasp of the woman next to her. She'd sabotaged her own chance of grabbing it.

Well, well, well. She didn't want to be the next to get hitched. Even in his state of brewing arousal, he knew exactly why.

Danica was buzzed as the crowd finally started to thin well past midnight. Not buzzed on booze—it typically took three full glasses of wine, or four beers, or an impressive five bottles of hard lemonade to get her tipsy, and so far she was under the two-flute limit she'd set for tonight. No, she was all fuzzy in the head and aflutter in the tummy because a man with the most sexilicious body she'd ever seen—well, of course she remembered his feature in *ESPN The Magazine*'s Body Issue—had felt her up.

Unfortunately, it wouldn't happen again. She had other plans for Dex Harper.

Working the room toward the exit, she noticed the woman who'd been snuggled up to him a while ago was now dancing rather intimately with another man. Dex was still in the hotel…somewhere. Only minutes before she'd spotted several teens bombarding him for autographs and camera-phone snapshots.

In the hushed foyer, she felt her throat constrict but didn't break her stride as she approached Dex, who stood near the massive wall of windows. He watched her confidently, as though he'd known she'd come searching for him.

"There's a gal with a pink streak in her hair who's doing a little dirty dancing with one of the groomsmen."

"Samantha's my ex-girlfriend. I escorted her to the wedding as a favor. Who she dirty dances, or does anything else dirty with, isn't my territory." Dex raked his gaze from her hair to the stiletto torture instruments that doubled as designer shoes. "Know something, Danica? Your face says you don't give a damn, but your body language is telling me a different story."

"That's a crock of—"

"Save it for a man who doesn't know anything about nonverbal behavior. Four-year hitch at LSU. I picked up a thing or two in the psych program. And watching people's moves, predicting what they'll do next, is part of a quarterback's job. Communication's about a lot more than words."

She'd be lying through her teeth to say she wasn't drawn in by the glint of heat that made his pupils flare. Was his restraint as tight as a drum, like hers?

"When I said that Samantha's my ex, your shoulders relaxed and you got a little closer. Not much, but enough for me to notice. The exact moment I called you on it, you tensed up again."

Danica wouldn't play into this man's games. But she couldn't walk away, either. She had a plan to put into place—a plan that required his full cooperation. Time to disarm him with…what?

"Danica Blue." The hint of military formality in the thunderous voice just behind Danica had her swinging around. Ah, yes. The father of the bride. A decorated military veteran, Elroy "Captain" Smart was as take-charge and startlingly powerful as her own father. Meddling mothers and larger-than-life fathers were what she and Veda had right away discovered they'd had in common and, frankly, was what had cemented their instant friendship.

"The one and only," Danica greeted. "Are you enjoying yourself, Cap?"

"My wife and Veda would settle for nothing less than a legendary party. Give me my slippers and a crisp newspaper any day. But the smile on my girl's face is worth all this expense and more." Cap looked beyond Danica and gave Dex an assessing look. "Well. Dexter Harper. The Blue-Eyed Badass."

Please, Cap, keep your commentary to yourself just this once. Don't mention his stats, his reputation, his unemployment, my firing him. In fact, don't mention football at all....

At least, not before Danica got Dex to agree to her suggestions.

"You're taller in person." With nothing more, Cap walked on.

The good thing about the interruption was that it took Dex's attention off the subject of Danica's body language and what tales it was telling on her.

"You've been on my mind," she told Dex, her face schooled into a neutral expression. "Your career, your situation, to be exact. I have a solution."

"Unless you have an offer from the Slayers, I'm not interested." His words were so final, his baritone so deadly serious, that she almost flipped him off for dismissing her without first allowing her to propose the damn solution.

But she wasn't so easily discouraged. "A contract with another team can resurrect your career. You were not Mr. Congeniality on the Slayers. The temper, the fines, the disrespect for authority? How many times did your coach chew you out last season for going rogue and disregarding his plays?"

"Disregarding bullshit plays, you mean," he growled. "Yeah, America thinks I'm an arrogant dick, but the truth is that the plays I wouldn't follow are the ones that would've screwed the team worse than it already was. I'm talking about a hell of a lot more turnovers and injuries. I'm talking about shit that only makes sense now that we know there were players and coaches on the take." His eyes burned like blue fire, and there was almost no trace of the flirt who'd teased her on the terrace. "You weren't out there. You don't know, Danica. *I* know. So trust me."

"What you're wanting me to do…I just can't, Dex."

"Then step aside."

Danica stopped him with a hand on his sleeve, but when he wrenched back his arm, her fingers slipped. Somehow her hand tangled with his, and she gripped him tightly. "You kissed me," she whispered. "Why?"

"After what happened yesterday, it was driving me insane wanting to know how you'd respond if I touched you. There came an opportunity to put it to the test, and I took it."

So he'd been toying with her. She should shrug it off, not take it seriously…be glad he didn't want to start up something serious. It wasn't as if she would sacrifice an image makeover project for mixed-up feelings toward a man she couldn't realistically have a future with anyway. Dex shattered rules, made enemies and never apologized. Danica was an expert at pleasing people—Miss Customer Service. A sunny disposition, a few witty words and a confident attitude almost always turned things in her favor. When that didn't work, ball-busting usually did the trick.

A romantic association would only propel them toward disaster. "And were you satisfied with the results of your little test?"

"No. Because I want more."

Danica's chin snapped up, and she searched his eyes for the callous playboy, the hellion, the angry and jobless quarterback. What she saw was just a man, unmasked and bared to her.

Underneath the layers—the Ball Buster, the "celebrity" GM and the darling, never-step-outside-the-lines Blue daughter—she was just a woman, a woman with a death grip on her perfect mask.

"But people don't always get what they want. That's according to you, Danica."

"That's according to life. I just want to know what your game is, Dex."

"Football. That's my game."

Danica was so close to leaving it at that, but unfortunately, it wasn't in her nature. What good were charm and charisma if she couldn't exercise her talents?

"Alessandro Franco and his band of money-motivated idiots threw you under the bus. Your image is the least of the feds' and the league's concerns. They aren't in any rush to clean it up. So what's a man to do when no one believes the truth?" She glanced down at their joined hands, and at last let him go. Suddenly it felt as though she were missing something essential. "The best shot you have of playing this season is to start looking good to teams—now. Change their minds about you. Make them want you—no, *compete* for you. You've created a name for yourself in football, Dex. Unfortunately, that name is the Blue-Eyed Badass. *Fortunately,* you have me."

"Right. And what does a good girl like Danica Blue want to do with a badass like Dex Harper?"

Besides snagging them a suite and letting him put that silk tie to more creative use on her?

"I'd like to help change the way the world sees you," she said.

Dex gave an ironic chuckle. "It's going to take more than a character reference to get me back onto a field."

"No one said it'll be easy. But it's possible. Think of how many people still approach you for autographs and pictures. You're not the first NFL player to chase redemption. Jesus, you're not even the first quarterback. Athletes have crawled back into the media's good graces from steroid hell, sex drama, drug charges, prison stints—"

"And what can you do?"

"Clean up your rep. Get you in the right situations at the right times. Get your name on *SportsCenter* for the *right* reasons. Keep this in mind, though. The Las Vegas Slayers will not pursue you. My parents' decision on that matter is final." She sidled closer, not caring what he might read in her body language. She needed him to hear her, totally and completely. "You're not a Slayer anymore, Dex. I'm willing to help you move on. But only if you want me to."

A scatter of guests passed them, laughing and jostling. One of the polished women tossed an appreciative glance back at Dex. Reflexively, Danica blurted to him, "Call me. Uh…after you think about my offer. If you're down with it, we can chat further and go over the logistics then."

Danica recited her private number to him; then with great care she marched—not bolted—to the ballroom.

What the royal hell was that? "Call me"? "Logistics"? In ways that were puzzling, Dex appealed to her. It was insulting that he'd skipped her on the chain of command to get to her parents. Yet compassion overwhelmed her. It was inappropriate of him to kiss her neck. Yet she was *still* turned on. It was infuriating that her guard slipped every time she was with him. Yet the fact that he provoked the part of herself she kept hidden was intriguing.

It was foolish to even fantasize about getting hot with one of America's sexiest sports idols. Yet, part of her— the part that wanted to be foolish, craved the danger—was ready for flesh and heat.

Ready for Dex Harper, and all the trouble that would come with him.

Chapter 6

Martha was a friendly drunk. It was the only thing restraining Danica from shoving her sister onto a kitchen stool, pouring her a mug of sobering coffee and tearing her a new one when they arrived at her place after the wedding reception.

By two, she'd had enough of pretending to be comfortable in her pain-inflicting shoes, enough of circling and manipulating the truth when asked about Martha's whereabouts. After she had collected her sister and tried to discreetly guide her away from the hotel, Martha gave her the slip and Danica searched the parking lot twice in her Boxster before she located her, tipsily yucking it up with a group Danica didn't know and firmly doubted Martha knew, either.

Now, as Martha strutted toward the living room precariously in her tassel high heels, tossing random compliments as freely as one would Mardi Gras beads, Danica activated the security system.

"Every time I visit, I fall in love with this fancy, fabulous, freakin' fantastic house all over again. Three stories of gorgeousness. Get divorced and get a mansion. Guess that's an okay reward for a decade of being a good wife to a cheater. But me? It'd be more like 'get divorced and get a new man.' Even if I was thirty, like you, I wouldn't swear off men and sex and relationships." Martha hugged one of the massive columns that divided the open space between the formal living room and the great room. An abrupt yelp of laughter startled Danica, who'd been shocked stupid by her sister's intoxicated honesty. "D'you hear how many *F* words I just said?"

Yes. You forgot one, and I'd like nothing more than to say it to you right now....

Danica gave her a long-suffering smile. "Coffee, Martha?"

"Latte."

Making room for her sister to sit and nurse her caffeine shot, Danica set down her purse and bridesmaid bouquet and cleared off a corner of the kitchen's center island, which doubled as a workstation. After the divorce she'd, for all intents and purposes, converted the extravagant bells-and-whistles kitchen into another office, having found no reason to restrict herself to the actual home office when there was a marvelous Las Vegas property at her sole disposal.

She removed a catchall basket from a stool, freeing it so Martha could plop onto it, throwing one leg over the other. She'd slept the night away in a room at the Mandarin Oriental, and it showed. Her makeup had smeared; her finger wave had fallen, leaving her chin-length hair a cap of glossy, messy waves. Miraculously, she managed to appear outrageously fashionable, like a flapper who'd sneaked too much bathtub gin.

"I didn't give up men and sex, FYI."

"Oh, yeah. Ollie Johan, known as McSexy. Forgot about him, since you pretty much dumped him the second he rolled off of you."

Danica almost dropped the delicate mug she'd retrieved from the cupboard. "Vulgar much?"

"What I meant to say is, you ended things awfully quickly. So it's relationships that you've sworn off. Got it."

"What did relationships get me before, Martha?"

"Uh…a mansion?" Her sister lifted one shoulder, let it drop. "Too bad about it all. A big place like this ought to be filled with kids and memories and love. But the split with Marion's already tough enough without the hassle of custody arrangements, isn't it?"

And time to switch gears. Much to her parents' disappointment, she had never gotten pregnant. *Let's wait until we're both ready,* Marion had insisted whenever she'd toyed with the idea of weaning herself off the pill. Then he'd confessed to cheating on her, she'd declared their marriage over and, suddenly, he was ready to put a bun in her oven in the name of "compromise." Yeah, he'd give her a child and she'd get over the heart-twisting hurt of being played for a fool.

She had wanted a baby—still wanted one—but not that way. Not with a man she could no longer trust and was no longer in love with.

"I took the liberty of giving your date your apologies. Call him later. I'm sure he'll want to hear from you that you weren't feeling well." Danica efficiently worked the espresso machine, then set a steaming cup of frothy delight in front of her sister, who said something along the lines of "Oh, hail to the barista." "Remember, Martha.

You weren't feeling the best, that's all. Say anything else and it'll contradict what I told people. Expect plenty of thoughtful notes and courtesy calls."

Martha said nothing, so Danica continued talking as she set her bouquet in water to preserve the flowers another day. Her feet now experienced a dull ache, but some habits she'd acquired during marriage—such as keeping herself fully dressed until she was upstairs in complete privacy, because she never knew when her husband would call an impromptu party—were difficult to break. "Check in with your friend Leigh Bridges, as well. Her father seemed only slightly pissed off, but they left without making a scene."

"And how pissed are you?"

Danica wanted to spare herself a ride on the blame-go-round. "Just sober up, and we're cool."

"So you say. When Ma's upset with one of us girls, she avoids looking us in the eye or just walks away. Even so, you just *know* she can see your every shortcoming. You're the same way."

"You know, a 'thanks, sis, for saving my ass' would've been nice. You're a publicist, for crying out loud, and you got yourself hammered as soon as the bar opened. Charlotte and I took care of things. Try being grateful, instead of bitching and moaning."

Martha stared into her latte. "You taught me that every action I take should have a reason behind it. Consider this. I was taking *my* liberty, by enjoying some bourbon without my mother and father hovering over me."

"Grow up, Martha. Start by finishing your latte and washing your face. You'll need to be up early and back at the Bellagio, if not the admin building, by the time Ma and Pop fly in this morning." Martha was staying with their parents in a villa at the hotel while their newly acquired lakefront mansion was in its final stages of renovation. At

Marshall and Temperance's insistence, Martha would be moving in right along with them, taking up her own wing but still under their roof.

"Okay, whoa. Put the brakes on the judgmental train." Martha hopped off the stool. "The only surprise is that you and Lottie even noticed me at the reception. She and Nate were so into each other. You and Dex Harper were cozied up."

"Not quite."

"*Quite.* I didn't sleep through the entire reception. I saw you two standing so close, whispering…about what, anyway?"

"You shouldn't drunk-spy on folks. He and I were talking sports. You and I are talking about *you.*"

Martha sighed. "I had too much to drink at your friend's wedding. Fine, sorry. But I was still wearing pigtails and playing with Barbie dolls the last time you rescued me from anything. I've learned to rescue myself since then, and I'm doing great without you getting involved."

"What have you rescued yourself from? Does Charlotte know? She's accused me of not even knowing you. Is that true?"

"I'm not doing this, Danica. Thanks for giving me a place to sleep. I'll camp out on the couch and will be out of your house by sunrise."

Danica sighed, exasperated. Her sister was already dashing out of the kitchen before she could think of some way to smooth the situation. She should've known better than to go this route with Martha, who was already rather sensitive without the enhancement of alcohol.

After some minutes of viewing *SportsCenter* game-day highlights on the kitchen television, she pressed the remote's power button and checked on Martha, still in her designer outfit, deeply asleep on the living-room sofa, like an all-partied-out princess. Danica was draping a blanket over her when the doorbell rang.

Glancing at the nearest clock, she rushed to the front door before the caller could ring again and risk waking her sister. Who'd have gotten through the privacy gate but didn't have a house key?

Marion. She'd changed the house locks but hadn't gotten around to updating the gate's security code.

"You shouldn't be here at this hour, Marion," she said, opening the door to him. To herself she quipped that she saw him more often now than she had during the entire last year of their marriage. Already, too many times to count, he'd shown up with one excuse or another—he'd left behind an important possession, he had to ask her a question, he wanted to show her how to manage the fuse box. It was a routine she was done with but hadn't yet figured out how to shut down. Their marriage was officially over, but they'd been ingrained in each other's lives for ten years. No, she didn't want a marriage of betrayal and nights of wondering where he was. But she hadn't expected change to hit her quite so hard.

"Whoever heard of a bridesmaid not having a date to her best friend's wedding?" Marion's smile, the attractive deep-dimpled grin that crinkled his eyes at the corners— like hers—had charmed her to goo every day of their marriage. Even at the end, on the days she hated him for forcing her to restart her life without the man she was supposed to grow old with, all he had to do was smile at her that way, and she was sunk.

But now it was only a smile.

Something else had changed between them, and it scared her a little. "Shh. Keep it down, please."

"Why? Who's here?" In a flash the smile transformed into a hard frown, and he walked farther into the house, leaving the aroma of fresh cologne in his wake. "You hooked up with somebody?"

"My sister's here, asleep. And if I had hooked up with somebody, it sure isn't any concern of yours." Danica gave him an impatient glare. "Come into the foyer. I really don't want to wake her up, and you're not staying."

Marion didn't protest. In the foyer, he let his gaze coast over her. How many times had he stood in front of her—with his bald head, richly dark skin and those tailored clothes that reflected all his hard-won success as a hip-hop/R&B music producer—and watched her with satisfaction in his eyes? How many times had it thrilled her to know that he approved of her? Why didn't it matter anymore? "You look amazing in that dress, Danni."

"Veda's choice. She has good taste. I'll let her know you think so, too." Danica gestured to him. "And you. You, old friend, look like a man whose bros let him know that his ex was alone at a wedding. What, did someone call you when I left the hotel so you could time your arrival perfectly?"

"You should've asked me to escort you."

"My ex-husband?" There were some people who could go to a wedding with an ex, but Danica and Marion weren't like that. A year apart hadn't neutralized the animosity and hurt feelings. "I shouldn't have let you in."

"Joke, right?" Another flash of his grin. "We're cool, aren't we?"

"I'm getting on fine without you. But thanks for thinking of me."

Marion shook his head. "I will love you for the rest of my life, Danni. Don't go thinking that'll change because we signed some papers last year."

"But you're not *in* love with me. That changed before we signed the papers." She forced her expression into one that was casual—impassive. "Dredging this all up again is rooting us in a place we shouldn't be. We're different now, Marion. You're music and BET and MTV. I'm sports and ESPN. We've got separate lives. Let's live them."

"Be out," he said, pointedly sidestepping everything she'd just said. He jerked down the door handle. "Just watching over you, Danni. You're a good woman."

"Tell me something I don't know."

Conflicted, Danica watched him depart to his souped-up Oldsmobile. Should she curse him for swooping in to remind her of how much easier life would be if things hadn't changed? Or thank him for reaffirming that easier wasn't the same as better?

Door shut, locked and secured again, she returned to the kitchen to boot up her laptop and review the reports she'd been sent. In a few hours she'd be expected to show up at the office, up to speed on every detail, from injuries to in-game performance.

Her cell phone rang. She made a dash for it before the sound could carry to the living room and awaken Martha and quickly silenced it.

Probably Marion calling to rub acid into her emotional wounds. She held up the phone, ready to press the ignore button, but the number on the display gave her pause.

"Hello?"

"Hello, Danica."

Right away, she was slung into the exquisite moments on a hotel terrace with Dex Harper kissing her neck, whispering against her skin, teasing her breast.

It occurred to her then that she hadn't much right to ream out her younger sister for not exhibiting model behavior at the reception. Martha was twenty-two and had drunk a bit too much, loosening her inhibitions. Danica was thirty and had had all her wits and sobriety about her when she let the quarterback she'd fired touch her in ways most men wouldn't dare. Maybe it was because he was as intoxicating as any liquor.

"You know, Dex," she said, "men have gotten a bad rap for waiting too long to call a woman."

"When we want to call a woman, we don't wait. Is your offer still on the table?"

"It is."

A pause. "You sound sad," he said softly.

"Ah. And you have experience with sad women?"

"Plenty," he said, not sounding proud at all. Just how many female hearts had he broken on his way to football glory? she wondered.

"Good to know. But you called me for a reason, and it ought to have something to do with what I can do for your career. So, did you decide?" She sensed hesitation. "Okay, Dex. How about this? Let's, for the rest of this call, put everything on the table. No holding back, no strategies. If you're going to take me up on my offer, then you'll need to trust me. And if I'm going to stick my neck out for you, I'll need to trust you."

At least somewhat. I trust no man completely. Not anymore.

Danica cleared her throat, forcing herself to focus on her project rather than whether he was still dressed in his suit…or dressed at all. "Change isn't easy, Dex. You imagined putting on a red-and-silver uniform this season, eventually retiring as a Slayer and making yourself a legend. But just because you want to be safe and settled somewhere doesn't mean that's how things are going to be."

"Safe and settled? Are we still talking about me, or the bridesmaid who ducked for cover when a bouquet was about to land in her hands? I saw you. I heard what your friend said to you earlier."

"I'm divorced. It's an adjustment. But what in life stands

still, anyway?" If she couldn't keep the quaver out of her voice, she'd have to end the call.

She didn't want to do that. It was ridiculously late, she was tired and frustrated with the world, but she didn't want to lose this connection. "Meanwhile, you didn't seem to mind that your ex found somebody."

"Samantha and I never loved each other, or anyone else."

"Must feel nice, to spare yourself that kind of hell."

"You say *nice*. Others say *empty*."

Danica fell silent, and was still considering this when he said, "I don't know how to trust that somebody else has my back. Going into this, please don't expect me to."

"Then you'll do it?"

"I want to play this season. If you can make it happen, then the answer's yes."

Victory! "We'll get started ASAP. No time to waste. But there're some rules. Rule number one—no pursuing a gig with the Slayers. Rule two—no going behind my back. Rule three is the most important. No more of that 'distract her with sex' stuff."

"Distract?"

"You look at me, and I get hot. When you touched me, I didn't want you to stop. I forget who I am, forget what makes sense." Her fingers moved to the nape of her neck, to where she thought she could still feel the press of his mouth. If she continued in this direction, they'd be in phone-sex territory. "It's pointless to build each other up if we won't do anything about it. Which we won't. This needs to be a professional relationship. Sex would only be trouble."

"I can't figure you out."

"Because I don't want to be figured out. When I do, I'll send a mass email."

"Go ahead. Make the rules, Danica." His pitch lowered; her blood rushed. "But I've got a habit of breaking rules. Just remember that."

Call of duty. It was the only explanation Marion Reeves could assign to what he was doing. Patrolling the hushed street, he circled twice in his vintage Oldsmobile before idling in front of his ex-wife's house longer than what was necessary—or sane, if he was going to be real about it. Performing a visual sweep of what could be seen of the three-storied house beyond its privacy gates, for twenty minutes—no, thirty now, his Rolex enlightened him—was unforgivable. At least, that's how Danica might call it if she got the impulse to walk out her front gate and found him stationed on the street. She wasn't in danger, was involved in nothing that would warrant anyone's surveillance.

The way she'd see it, there was no logical reason for the man who'd married her, then slept his way into a divorce that had been more than fair considering what she could've walked away with, to take up so much space in her life. Guilt was in control; he was simply a vessel. It clawed at his insides, sickened his heart, punished him for starting up a life that didn't include her.

What did it matter that when they'd gotten together, he and Danica had been nothing more than children in love with the bragging rights that came with being married and responsible for uniting two strong, respectable families? She'd believed in the dream up until the night he'd had to wake her up. Honesty, coming clean, was supposed to be a humane end to the suffering.

All it did was crush the heart of the woman who'd stuck by him through college and careers and red-carpet fame. And since he'd been the cause of it, it was up to him to fix the mess he'd made.

Somehow. Dragging his gaze across the top of the house again, noting that there were still lights on and figuring she was drenching herself with work, he exhaled. Divorced for a year, and still he wasn't free. He'd thought that he couldn't be with her. Damn, he couldn't be without her, either. But she didn't want him. She'd been insisting that for months, pushing him away, but now he accepted it as true. The difference shone in her eyes. Danica was an expert at disguise when it suited her purposes, but he'd known her intimately for so long that he could always find the truth in her eyes.

She was longing for someone else.

He tried not to let that suspicion bother him. But every time he got close to letting himself forget how he'd hurt her, or think that it was safe to move on, he'd be reminded that he had a duty to watch over the woman he'd married.

Marion aimed a vicious glare at his phone as it vibrated on the dash. "Not now. Don't call me again tonight," he growled to the caller. Stabbing the power button, he tossed the phone into a cup holder, stomped the accelerator and jetted down the street.

Danica would rush to the front windows, and stare through the darkness for the source of the noise. But he'd be long gone.

Chapter 7

Checkmate. Danica had wanted to say the word to her father since before she'd stopped believing in Santa Claus. Her mother wasn't a worthy opponent at chess; Danica had defeated her at age nine and soon lost interest in challenging her. Tem didn't seem to mind, as she'd preferred playing pool since her beauty-pageant years. Over twenty years and hundreds of matchups later, Marshall was still the chess champion of the Blue household. He held back his superb skill for no one. While her sisters weren't as interested, Danica was like Captain Ahab hunting Moby Dick. She couldn't let it go.

To her, the relentless ache to be victorious was about more than chess. With each loss, Danica was reminded that she could be predicted, outsmarted...bested. Winning would be a rite of passage, proof that she was mentally strong enough to do what neither of her sisters was capable of—beating Marshall.

Danica shifted in the Gothic striped visitor's chair that she'd pushed up to her desk, second-guessing her move as she looked across the antique chessboard to her father. You'd think by now she would've figured out how to read him. But no. Marshall was relaxed, his jacket over the wide back of her executive chair, his skin glowing a dark sienna as he sat behind her desk with that same hard-eyed, frowning expression that intimidated strangers and loved ones alike.

He looked bored as hell.

Today, Marshall and Tem had called a press conference in the aftermath of their starting QB's being pulled late in Sunday's game. Their head coach, Kip Claussen, had shown common sense in sitting out Brock Corday, who'd aggravated the rotator-cuff injury he'd suffered during this season's training camp. As Danica had gathered from reports and the films, Brock had had nothing more to give in the game and would be better off rested and then prepped for the next game. Their second-string backup had performed well enough to lead the Slayers to a win—and that's what mattered.

The media weren't easy to pacify and were hungry for details about the currently undefeated team's stability. Inviting them for a midweek Q&A at the stadium had been Martha's suggestion—which had, as was typically the case, been batted away. Then, as an afterthought, Marshall and Tem had reconsidered and given her mere hours to prep the staff and organize the chat. She'd pulled it off, though not without first throwing a few things in her office, then recruiting Danica and a janitor to clear away the shattered glass.

A pre–press conference chess match had been Marshall's idea—something to occupy his idle time until he,

Tem and Danica would join the head coach and their starting quarterback in the pressroom.

As with every match with Marshall Blue as the opponent, Danica felt it was less of a game and more of a test.

Tem swept into the office, all Chanel No. 5 and Diane von Furstenberg, holding an amber vase. Placing it on a shelf, she then buzzed about the room, rearranging knick-knacks. "Danica, won't you let your mother redecorate this place? I feel the need to say a prayer before I come in here." She made a show of poking a moon lamp shade to see if it would sprout fangs and snap. "I do love this picture, though."

Danica observed her mother trace the frame of the coloring-book art she'd held on to for years. Danica's crayon strokes were neat, careful. Charlotte's were heavy-handed and sloppily outside the lines. Martha's were off the page.

Tem turned away from the art, and her gaze stalled on her daughter's crossed legs. "Marshall, did I ever wear leather pants with zippers up the ankles? Or a blouse that leaves so little to the imagination?"

"No," Marshall answered, prying his attention from the chessboard to smile slowly at Tem, "but it's not too late to start."

The idea of classic, couture Tem rocking skyscraper stilettos, leather pants and a sleeveless button-down made Danica giggle. The in-your-face getup was for the late night of barhopping she'd promised her assistant, Lilith. But after work and before bar stop number one was the private get-together she'd been looking forward to all day. She'd stayed up to much too long talking to Dex on the phone after the reception, but somehow, in those quiet predawn hours, it hadn't mattered.

"Who's the leather for?" Marshall asked. "The press?"

Tem moved so light-footedly that she practically floated

across the room to hover over his shoulder. Without even thinking, Marshall brought his hand up to clasp her arm lovingly. "Or a date, Danni? I heard that you had no escort to Veda's wedding."

"Who told you that?"

Marshall made a move. "Checkmate."

"Marshall, you shouldn't annihilate your girls in chess," his wife advised. "It's not good for their self-confidence."

"I certainly don't want him to let me win, Ma."

"About your leather pants…"

Danica smothered the urge to roll her eyes. "I dress for no one's satisfaction but my own these days. I'm going clubbing with Lilith. We're meeting up at the Marquee at midnight. But before then, I'm meeting Dex Harper."

"Harper? Is this about the QB position?" Marshall demanded. "Corday sits out the fourth, we call a press conference and now Harper wants in with the GM?"

"No." She helped put away the chessboard because it gave her a fantastic excuse to avoid eye contact.

"Then, what could he possibly want with you?" Tem asked.

Well, damn. Obviously the woman who couldn't keep her husband satisfied couldn't hook a pro-football playboy, right? Marion had women accosting him with seduction in mind on a daily basis. Dex wasn't any different, unless every one of the paparazzi's photos showing him with a barrage of women was a trick of Photoshop.

"It's what I want with him," Danica said brightly. "I think he's being truthful about what went down with Alessandro Franco and the team. The man got screwed, he wants to play and he needs a push in the right direction. I'm going to help him look good for another team. Free advice for him. A can't-miss project for me."

"Dex has been clear about getting back what he says

was taken from him," Tem said. "You know what he wants from us. You also know what we want from him. The names—"

"Ma. Pop. I'm not asking him for names. We should start interviewing all of last season's Slayers again. I'm talking about interrogating. Grilling. Because we're not using Dex to sift through our roster." At Tem's series of blinks, and Marshall's twitch of a frown, she softened her approach. "We wouldn't want outsiders to get the impression we need someone no longer affiliated with our franchise to help us manage it. It'll show shallow faith in our staff and in your competence."

This was met with nods and murmurs of agreement. And back on their good side, she was. Close call. Thankfully she'd figured out by now how to push back without them quite realizing it. While everything seemed to be changing around Danica, the one constant she clung to was her relationship with her parents. She would never jeopardize one of the few things in her universe that still made sense.

"The trade deadline is right on our asses," her father said. "No time to beat around the bush with last season's men. Get Tem the contracts of each player by tomorrow start of day, Danica. The three of us will make some decisions in the p.m."

Which meant tonight's barhopping would be cut short if Danica intended to sleep before gathering the material and delivering it to her employers. "Yes, sir. Anything else?"

"Get it across to Harper that he won't have his hand on any part of this organization."

About that. He's already had his hand on me, but neither of you would believe me if I told you. Keeping that snarky nibble to herself, Danica made a grab for her purse as two firm raps sounded at the door.

She swiveled toward it, grateful for the interruption. Opening the door, she met Kip Claussen with a benign, reveal-nothing smile. Working closely with him, she knew more about the head coach than she knew about any of her nonfamily colleagues. The consequence of that was on the flip side, Kip knew a great deal about her, too, so throwing him off seeing what she didn't want him to was that much more difficult.

Fresh from a practice, he was all hard-nosed coach in jeans, a team-issue sweatshirt, a ball cap and possibly the tenth pair of designer sunglasses she'd seen him wear since first meeting him months ago. The man was notorious for taking out his frustration on his eyewear. "Got a minute, Danica?"

"For you? Always." Danica snagged the opportunity to escape Marshall and Tem's drill-sergeant approach to management.

Kip wasted not a moment as they took to the hallway that was peppered with business-casual front-office staff, IT experts in graphic tees and frayed jeans with ID tags dangling from neon-colored lanyards, and catering staff in snazzy jackets decorated with the Slayers Club Lounge logo. "The passing game was shit today."

Not what Danica wanted to hear. "Give me the injury update. What do Whittaker and the other trainers advise?"

Pulling off the cap and dragging a hand carelessly through his short golden hair, Kip grimaced. "Brock Corday's iced and wrapped. He won't be at the press conference. Rest today. Light on practice tomorrow."

At the elevators she punched the down button. "And Sunday? Can he be relied on to start?"

"He's probable. If his form and accuracy straighten out in tomorrow's practice, then yes, he'll start. It's a slight aggravation, Danica. Not nearly as severe as the original injury. Still, Corday wants more strength than he has, and if he pushes himself too damn far, he's going to go from starting to warming a bench. Marshall, Tem and I discussed this already, but I want to stress to you that it'd be a good idea to give our second and third guys more snaps."

There was no other feasible option if Brock Corday couldn't play. The Slayers had spent economically, considering the names they'd acquired. A rising star like Corday, not to mention highly sought-after draft picks, hadn't been cheap. Danica's concentration was split between the ball club's budget, contract clauses and acquisitions as she preceded Kip into the pressroom. Taking a seat at the table, she closed her hand over the mic in front of her and meaningfully raised an eyebrow at the head coach. Today's developments would not be made public.

The live broadcast began once Marshall and Tem got seated onstage. As at the start of every press conference, they both sized up the gathering of columnists, reporters and photographers, and reminded Danica of a king and queen observing their subjects. Would that make her a princess or a lady-in-waiting?

A sportswriter from the *Las Vegas Sun* directed his question to Marshall. "Brock Corday was benched in the fourth. What's the likelihood that he'll play Sunday?"

"He'll play." Marshall's imposing stature and the buoyancy in his voice lent Danica comfort. Her whole life, he'd slain her every dragon and had been the one to emphasize the importance of success. Anything she wanted could be hers if she found the right way to go after it. She believed it, believed in everything he and her mother preached. If he was confident that Corday would play, then her worries stopped there.

"It's a preseason injury that's still healing," her father was reiterating. "For optimum results, and for the longevity of Corday's career, he'll rest when he needs to. Twenty–ten score. I think we can all agree that Cruz Shankman tied up the game nicely. Next." Marshall jabbed a finger toward a news reporter at the far left of the room.

"Question for the general manager."

Danica sent the reporter a coy grin. He faltered for a moment, backlit by the flashes of cameras, but that fleeting hesitation was all she needed to know she could handle whatever he dished out.

"How satisfied are you with TreShawn Dibbs?" the reporter asked, referring to the kicker Danica had hired in spite of his checkered past and the firestorm of talk about his prior experiences with performance-enhancement substances.

"Since the season opener he's abided by the terms of his contract with our team and he's maintained one hundred percent accuracy on all field goals. Who wouldn't be satisfied with stats like that?"

That didn't stop him from persisting, though. "Even you have to admit it was a risky move to acquire a player suspected of so many transgressions."

"Dibbs is healthy and giving our franchise the results we want. What would football be without risky moves? You never know what action I'm going to take next. Don't ruin all the excitement by trying to predict me."

This earned a wave of laughter, and the reporter blushed as though embarrassed to have even broached the subject.

The next question was for the head coach. "How might new discoveries in the Alessandro Franco investigation affect your roster?"

"Ask me again *after* more discoveries are made, and you'll get a better answer," was Kip's laid-back reply. "Right now I can say that this club has a well-prepared second string. Each individual on our team is an asset, but no one's indispensible. We all like to think we're irreplace-able, but at the end of the day we're components of a team, and the team's success trumps everything."

Amid the murmurs and camera flashes was someone waving a plastic object toward the stage. A member of security hovered before Kip signaled for the object to be tossed to him.

Danica laughed as he showed her the bobblehead before setting it on the table beside his water glass.

"Ah, damn, my wife warned me that these hit the mar-ket," he said on a groan. "I didn't think anyone would have the balls to give me one."

"Do you think it's a good likeness?" Danica asked, pick-ing up the novelty toy to hold next to his face. The media ate up the banter, cheering in approval of the figure that exaggerated Kip's wide, lopsided grin and the dimples that bracketed his mouth. It held a clipboard in one hand and half a pair of sunglasses in the other.

"To who? Me or Richie Cunningham?"

"That can't *possibly* represent Kip Claussen," Tem countered in good humor. "The bobblehead nods. Kip never nods. He's one of the most disagreeable men I've ever met." Mimicking a prize model, she gestured to her husband with a graceful flourish. "And he's the other."

Danica looked toward her father, saw him give an ever-so-slight nod of satisfaction. She'd handled herself well, and for him this press conference had just become another victory. Checkmate.

How the hell did they do it? Dex pushed his Corona across the bar with a forefinger and motioned for another. He was at the Hard Rock Hotel's sports bar with his eyes glued to the prerecorded broadcast at Slayers Stadium play-ing out on a plasma screen. He had to give the Blues and

Kip Claussen credit for twisting what was going to be a painful press conference into a goddamn variety show.

Danica Blue's blatant—at least to him—manipulation of the reporter who'd started up about TreShawn Dibbs had set the tone. There was something in the way she leaned in, with one shoulder forward and a black-painted fingernail drawing up and down the neck of her mic, that compelled him to stare at her. Even as she appealed to every male fiber of his being, he saw through her act. He couldn't define what was hidden behind the clever flirtation and ballsy attitude she flaunted to the press, but there was more to her than a beautiful face, a smart mouth and a honeyed voice that would sound so good moaning his name.

The woman on-screen appeared too carefree to be sad in the depths of night, too self-involved to spare time on a man who'd promised her nothing in return. But Dex knew better. He knew that she'd been home alone, nursing some private wounds, after her friend's wedding. He knew that when she'd given her word to help him get back onto the field, she meant it.

Fishing for a few laughs, throwing people off with a curve of her pillowy lips, were tactics, he realized. Watching her on television, as he waited for her to join him at the bar, was more about curiosity than anything else. She'd had the media snug in her back pocket since she'd hit the NFL scene, and today he'd wanted to observe how she went about transforming a pack of bloodthirsty lions into purring cats. At the close of the conference, all Dex had confirmed was that she was a mystery. And sexier than anyone had a right to be.

Dangerous, dangerous, dangerous. Maybe if his brain repeated it enough, his dick would get the message.

Fact was, he was skeptical that one woman could right his reputation, and he didn't want to take a roundabout route toward proving that he'd been a target. At eighteen, he'd chosen sports over a future in Oregon agriculture. The football field and all it represented had become his home, the team his family, the game his life. But his "family" had betrayed him, gutted him, and righting the wrong was something he couldn't walk away from.

If Slayers Stadium would never again be his home, then so be it, so long as another team valued his potential. So long as the Slayers franchise and the media regretted shutting him out.

Dex turned up the bottle for a deep swig, then swiveled around to put his back to the television. The move granted him a comfortable view of the bar—which was right away obstructed by a cluster of autograph-hungry fans. He might be unemployed, but to the people grinning and holding out objects for him to sign, he was still a Las Vegas Slayers quarterback, still jersey number eleven.

He accepted the Sharpie a bartender tossed him and in a blur signed a cell phone case, a napkin, a baseball cap, a handbag.

Then someone appeared on the fringes of the group. "Darn it. I don't have anything for you to sign. Poor, poor me."

He raised his eyes to the woman. Danica. Watching video footage of the press conference hadn't prepared him for the full effect of seeing her in leather pants that wrapped her long legs like a second skin, and a shirt that exposed her arms, shimmied over her breasts and brushed her hips.

"Yeah, you do. Want me to show you?"

"Go for it."

Dex got off the bar stool. Grasping her arm, he drew the pen over her skin, just above the bend of her elbow. He signed with pride, with a little cockiness in his stroke.

He then lowered his mouth as if to drop a kiss there, but gently blew across the ink.

Danica's laughter stole his attention. A no-holds-barred grin showed off a set of white teeth and wrinkled the outer corners of her eyes. "What a smart-ass!"

She turned to skim her surroundings, and the lightness of the moment fell away. Patrons craned their necks to spy from the bar and the edges of booths. "Busier than I thought it'd be on a Wednesday."

"Rethinking being with me in public?"

"On the contrary. *Public* means I've got nothing to hide. *Private* means secrets. I have my secrets, Dex, but being here with you isn't one of them."

She zeroed in on the nearest television. Tension tightened her shoulders as the sports analyst on-screen promised a rundown of league-wide developments after the commercial break.

"Saw the press conference. The bobblehead bit was genius."

"That wasn't a bit, Dex. It wasn't planned."

"Still took the heat off Claussen."

Danica planted a fist on her hip. "Claussen doesn't need anyone to take the heat off him. If he did, he wouldn't be our head coach. Don't knock his abilities. In fact, you would've worked well with him—" Catching herself, she stopped, and he could damn near see the tension strapping itself on to her like armor.

No. He wouldn't accept more of that. Damn the masks, the pretenses, the hiding. Screw everything that took away the woman who'd let him sign her arm and had laughed freely for him. The hard-shelled persona was nothing more than a piece of clothing—something to project an image.

She'd dropped that persona once, and now that he'd seen what was underneath, he wouldn't settle for a facade again.

"Cards on the table. Remember that? Say what's on your mind. I like you better when you do."

"Then let's take this talk someplace else," she suggested, with another glance at the television. "A place without all-sports TV?" She pointed to his Corona. "I'll buy your beer."

"My beer's paid for." Dex tossed the Sharpie onto the counter, then added an extra twenty to an already generous tip. "So make it a tequila. I know a place."

One corner of her mouth inched up. Not a full-on smile, but close enough to give him a sting of pleasure, like a woman's teeth to his shoulder. "Not *your* place, 'cause that's not happening."

"Don't worry, Danica. I'm abiding by your rules. It's a public place, but private enough to talk, and there's no sports TV. The question is, will you be okay with a situation you don't have complete control over?" He turned, and there she was, at his side, with a spark in her eyes to go with that bounce in her step.

"I'll follow you there. I'm not getting in your car. What would people think?" She gave him a grab-the-man-by-the-loins wink. "Besides. I trust my Boxster to no one."

She was as brilliant at evasion as he was at throwing a football. But her resistance intrigued him when it should've frustrated him. He let her exit the bar ahead of him, warning himself that sooner or later he'd regret letting recklessness take over. For every reason he had to step back from her, he was shot with the urge to get even closer. His bloodstream was damn near poisoned with the want to know her, touch her—

Getting into his Corvette, he slammed the driver's door. The sudden noise jarred his thoughts for a slice of a moment, and he was glad for it. As pretty and complex as

Danica Blue was, she was also the woman who'd cut him from his team and had smiled while doing it.

In his rearview mirror, Dex could see her car. Occasionally a traffic light or the twin beams of his brake lights streaked across the front of her vehicle, revealing her behind the windshield. Head bopping, lips moving, one hand slapping the top of the steering wheel.

At the Luxor she was all cool, serious businesswoman as she met him at the entrance with an expectant frown.

"On the road, were you singing in your car?"

The only sign that she was flustered by the question was a quick succession of blinks, which only drew his focus to the sexy catlike shape of her eyes. "I was." She wiggled her fingers at the building. "You brought me to the Luxor to talk?"

"Our stop's the very low-key lounge inside. Been here before?"

"Haven't had the pleasure."

Pleasure and discretion were what the exclusive, intimate lounge provided. That he was the man introducing her to this place and the unspoken possibilities teased his ego.

"I'm not really acquainted with the Vegas club scene, Dex."

The surprises kept coming. Her ex-husband was constantly in the news, photographed at parties and clubs that some men would give their left nut to have access to. Her younger sister was a hard partier. He'd come across that fact firsthand at a casino some weeks ago, had caught a glimpse of Martha Blue unplugged—loud, freewheeling and belligerent—and he'd muttered good luck to any man masochistic enough to try to catch a fireball like that. Yet Danica, the woman who ditched her inhibitions in the privacy of her car to sing along to the radio, wasn't a club-goer.

"I'm going out tonight, though," she continued as he led her inside, "so I can't stay past midnight."

For these few moments, it was just the two of them journeying through the dimly lit halls. So he asked. "What happens after midnight? Something turns into a pumpkin?"

She chuckled. "I'm impressed with your knowledge of fairy tales."

All thanks to my kid sister. To be fair, Erin was an adult now. But after almost fifteen years of estrangement, what he remembered most about his life as an older brother were the moments he should've appreciated but hadn't. The times she pestered the hell out of him to read her a story, ran to him for protection from playground bullies, tagged along when he'd finally gotten a license and all the freedom that had come with it.

Erin had sent him a letter his rookie season in New York—nothing more than a "I hate you for not telling Mom and me that your dreams came true" note that had slipped past the team's publicity department in a batch of fan mail. Because he'd still been grieving his father's death and hadn't figured out a way to freeze his heart against his remaining family, he'd hung on to that contact. Playing for a team across the country, he'd been limited to an occasional visit home and sizable checks to support his mother and Erin. His mother's death had left Erin as his only connection to his past. She was his one chance to do right by his family; his parents had depended upon him to protect her.

To ensure that she got an education and never had to leave home, he paid for Erin's college in Corvallis and purchased their family's cherry orchard and turned it over to her. Keeping her in Oregon and himself in Las Vegas was for her own good, even though she'd been stubbornly putting herself in the public eye with a gig posting home design and organization videos on YouTube. He was giv-

ing her the safe, out-of-the-limelight life his parents had
wanted for both Dex and Erin—the life he *hadn't* wanted.

They emailed regularly—or *had,* up until she'd gotten
word of his release from the Slayers.

"Come home," she'd begged. "Come back to the farm
for a while. Or I can come to Las Vegas and stay with you.
We've got to find some way out of this mess."

No, he wasn't interested in going back to Gunner, Oregon, with his tail tucked between his legs. And letting
his small-town sister wander into the middle of a place
that was called Sin City for a reason was out of the damn
question. The emails and voice-mail messages that he'd left
unanswered were beginning to accumulate, but it seemed
the best way to deal with his sister was through silence.
Still, he'd hate himself if he lost the girl who'd looked up
to her big brother and believed in fairy tales.

"Nothing will turn into a pumpkin," Danica told him.
"But I'll owe someone an apology and a drink."

Ushering her through the lounge, he watched her take
notice of the candlelight, dark furniture, the DJ and the
scatter of high-roller guests who were too absorbed in conversation and heavy petting to toss up more than a glance.

"A guy someone?" he asked, sitting across from her at
a shadowed table.

Anyone could've picked up on the thin edge of jeal-
ousy in his words. Dex wanted to smack himself upside
the head for asking that question. Why should he care if
she had a date lined up?

"My assistant. I'm not seeing anyone," she answered,
with a hesitant smirk that spoke volumes. She was pleased
that he'd asked, but she knew she'd taken a risk in telling
him that she was single. "Uh, apparently, man-hunting is
more fun when women go in pairs."

"What type of man are you hunting for?"

"I'm *not*. And as for type…well, I never thought about it." She shifted with a nervous energy. "Been out of the dating loop for a while. Which I'm sure you know, if curiosity and easy access to Google got the best of you."

She almost had him there. Yes, he'd been tempted to do some online digging. But the bigger appeal was in discovering her through that push-pull that reeled him into a debate with her at every turn. They always seemed to be on the borderline of disagreement, and maybe he was crazy, but he liked it that way.

"I know you were married to Marion Reeves, and now you're not."

"God. It's not that simple."

"Then what is it?"

"I was in high school when I met Marion. I looked at him and saw this fairy-tale future. He was so charming. My parents were in his corner. Best of all, he wanted me. I graduated, married him right away. After ten years, it was over. The next guy I dated pursued me, and that was okay, except…I wasn't the one who made the move that matters. For me, the kiss—not a peck on the cheek, but a mouth-to-mouth kiss—changes things." Danica cleared her throat. "I think it's time for that tequila."

At the bar they knocked back a round of tequila shots, with salt and lime wedges. Then Danica let a mixologist talk her into a harvest-moon cocktail, which she took back to their table. Instead of reclaiming her seat, she took the one beside him, crowding him deliciously with that tight little body, rattling him with the sparkle of mischief in her smile. "Dex, your social life's as legendary as your NFL career. It's also a huge part of the image that the public sees. So let's talk about that. About your relationships."

"Irrelevant."

"Actually, no. We talked about mine, and my image is fine."

"Yeah, except I have a hell of a hard time believing you've been into just two guys your whole life."

"Those weren't my exact words. Might want to fix that selective listening thing if you want this—" she gestured from him to herself with an index finger "—to work out. My first crush happened when I was five."

"Give me a name. Or I won't believe you."

"Steve Perry. It's true. And for the past few years Blair Underwood's been looking really good to me. Now—" Danica gently nudged him with her shoulder, catching him with those inviting chocolate-brown eyes "—your turn. First crush. Current crush."

"All right. Marisa Tomei. Been sold on her since *My Cousin Vinny.*"

"Wow, the same woman for several years. You *can* commit."

"A Hollywood crush is one thing—"

"And reality is another. In reality, you don't commit. I get it—it's a choice. Your life's an open door to…let's see. Models. Actresses. Legions of beautiful fans. I'm not judging you," Danica added, the humor in her voice replaced with sincerity. "Just getting a clearer picture of Dex Harper, the man. That's the part of you in need of a reboot, because without it you can't resurrect Dex Harper, the pro quarterback."

"What is it about me that needs improvement, then, Danica?"

"Try to see this from the public's point of view. You want to be someone that average Joes might admire. Show the world that you're down-to-earth. A man who can be humbled, who deserves empathy, who's fun to be around. Your involvement with Habitat for Humanity would be a plus if your bad behavior didn't work against it. Appearing in gossip rags with a different model on your arm every week? Unleashing your temper every time a reporter asks you about the investigation? It tells people that you're a careless hothead. And people will love to hate you.

"Now that the feds and the league are wringing out Alessandro Franco, reporters are greedy for information. With them it comes down to competition. Ratings. Popularity. There's only so much you're at liberty to discuss, I realize that. But what's going to impact your future the most isn't what you say, but to whom you say it. Strategy."

"Manipulation," he countered. "Call it what it is."

"Perceive it however you wish. It's going to get you into a football uniform this season. Rethink the company you keep. Want to continue living it up with your hordes of friends, racking up models and actresses and groupies? Be more discreet about it."

Even before he was released from the Slayers, he'd grown weary of the one-night-stand routine. The women were different, but the situations always seemed the same.

The last woman he'd been with who hadn't been motivated by an opportunity to climb the social ladder, who'd proven to be a legitimate friend, was Samantha. But sex with Samantha came with more complications than benefits, and for the sake of their sanity, he'd drawn the line weeks ago. Regardless, it riled him up to have someone give him dating directions. Especially when she was the same woman who'd hijacked his dreams two nights in a row.

"The women I see aren't anyone's damn business, Danica."

"They are when you're famous. Your talent made you famous, even if being tracked by paparazzi and criticized by ESPN isn't what you signed up for when you entered

this league. I understand that more than you might believe, Dex, and I've come to accept that my life isn't my
own anymore. And this is coming from a GM, someone
behind the scenes who's not front and center on the field
or tied to endorsements."

Did she resent that her life wasn't her own anymore?
She didn't seem to. The media worshipped her. She fired
people with a smile on her face.

"That's just part of the biz. My sister Charlotte's as stub-
born as they come, loves to do things her way, but even
she had to learn that lesson."

"What about Martha? She's the publicist in the family.
Shouldn't she be the expert in spinning conversation?" *Instead of making herself the subject of it?*

"I taught Martha everything she knows. How she uses
her knowledge makes sense to only her." Danica drummed
her shiny black nails on the table before lacing her fingers.
"Let's go back to basics, Dex. You got into LSU with decent grades, some impressive SAT scores and, of course,
a canon of an arm. What happened before LSU?"

"Not much," he said stiffly. "Busted my ass doing what
I could to get recruited someplace far from Oregon. LSU
and going pro is all that mattered to me."

"Basics, Dex. Before Baton Rouge. All the time in Oregon, where you were born and raised, is just a blurb in
your file."

"Oregon's got nothing to do with my career."

"It has plenty to do with you, though. Your roots."

"I'm a farmer's son. My father was the first to put a
football in my hands. He taught me the game, but he meant
for my career to revolve around our cherry orchard and
carpentry. Using my skills to help others—that's where
Habitat for Humanity came in. That was his path, his father's. Tradition."

"Why wasn't it your path?"

"I didn't see myself in agriculture or a town that's so quiet a man can lose his mind. I wanted exactly what New York and Las Vegas gave me—noise, women, fast cars, an open bar at any time of night. More than anything, I wanted to make it pro and prove that talent like mine shouldn't be wasted as some farmer's hobby."

"What'd your family think about that?"

"There was a falling-out. I started going into the city, hanging with guys who dreamed big about having a shot at the NFL. My abilities raked in a lot of attention. Friends, cold beer, girls. It all started to come so easily. Life was good."

"It didn't stay that way, though, Dex. What happened when life stopped being 'good'?"

"My parents saw me as growing up into a man they didn't want in their lives. The city was changing me fast, they said. When LSU came knocking, I had a choice—see where football would take me or stay put. Fall into line, or leave. They gave me no leeway. I made my choice."

Danica was silent for a long moment, and there was nothing but the pound of music between them. "Who'd you leave behind?"

"Mom. Dad. Younger sister."

"None of them ever came to a game or talked to you?"

"Just my sister, Erin. Dad died when I was still at LSU." He'd died before Dex could make himself be man enough to go home, apologize and shake hands with the man he'd wanted to be proud of him.

"And never your mother?"

"She watched my games on TV. I never asked her for more than that. Danica, she died my first year with the Slayers."

"I saw nothing in your file about that."

"Wasn't relevant to the game and what I could do for my team in the play-offs. I asked the head coach and Alessandro Franco for leave so I could bury Mom and be there for my sister. They said no. I was told to say a prayer for my mother and play. This was the test to see how committed to the team I was."

"You played those games. You went to the Super Bowl," Danica said softly.

"Yeah. That's how committed I was. What did that commitment earn me?"

"I'm sorry for you. I—I just find it heartbreaking."

"I don't want that," he told her. "The 'I'm sorry' and the pity."

She pushed her drink to the center of the table. "But to be alone? I can't imagine not having my family to count on. My parents—they're my rock."

"That's great for you, Danica. That's not my life."

"It's your past, so it matters. The farm, the carpentry? Habitat for Humanity? These are things you care about. It's what we need to sell."

"Sell? As if my family, my history, the secrets of my life that matter most are commodities? No. Make that *hell, no.* I never agreed to exploit my family. My little sister's all I have left, she's safe and sound in Oregon, and I'm not going to drag her down with me. Leave it alone, Danica."

"Don't you want to be humanized to the public? I knew there was more to you than your stats, this scandal and your collection of women."

"I'm finding it hard to think the public's entitled to that kind of transparency. Even you're not an open book—unless it's true that you get a thrill out of firing people and living as though life's a game of *Minesweeper.*"

"Minesweeper?"

"Strategizing, thinking carefully about the next move, always afraid of detonating something."

Danica's eyebrows pulled together. "I prefer *goal-oriented*," she snapped. "And for the record, I have never gotten a thrill taking someone's job away. I didn't enjoy cutting you from the team. That's the truth." She appeared to want to stop talking, stop sharing, but the words surged forward anyway. "*Minesweeper?* I have a heart. It belongs to my family and friends and Faith House."

Faith House. He knew that she'd founded the organization, but not that part of her heart belonged to it. "What about the rest of your heart? Is that reserved?"

"There's nothing left. I have a very full life, Dex." She then softened her face into a gentle expression that would make a killer photograph. Damn, she was good. "I get zero financial or social gain out of helping you. This is just my advice. Think about it before you reject me."

"I'm rejecting the suggestion that I 'sell' where I come from. I'm not rejecting you…or what goes through my head when I'm with you. Even though the devil knows I should."

She turned fully toward him, wetting her lips as he reached to stroke the scribble of ink on her arm.

"Make your move, Danica."

"I don't do *bad,* Dex. Never have. This…what we're walking into…would be beyond bad." She shook her head, as though confused. "We can't expect a real relationship. Slayers GM here."

"I'm not a Slayer."

"Because *I* released you. Aside from that, we argue about damn near everything. I don't even know if you like me. Or if I like you. There are lines we shouldn't cross. Remember rule number three?"

"Uh-huh. Is that working out for you?" She was leaning in but holding herself in check. It took Herculean effort to stop touching her, but he had to let her initiate the next contact.

"No."

He watched her mouth slowly murmur the word. Whether he kissed her or she kissed him, he didn't care. He wanted to taste that mouth, indulge in her flavor. But he wasn't going to compromise her that way. Their table was private; the club wasn't.

"Do you want to leave?"

"No," she said again.

His pulse drummed in his ears as she strapped one of those slender, leather-clad legs across his lap. The weight of it settled over his crotch. She dragged her leg back and forth across his lap, quickening her efforts as his cock hardened to concrete.

"Can a man think rationally when a woman touches him like this?" Nimbly she replaced her leg with her palm. Molding her fingers to his shape, she let her nails scratch his pants. The pressure glided along his shaft, base to tip, again and again. The pleasure was his to take, but she looked caught in fascination.

How far would she take him? How much longer would she tantalize his body and his restraint?

Danica's fingers crawled to his fly. A buckle unfastened, a button twisted free, a zipper lowered with a whisper. Eyes on his, she swirled her tongue over her fingertips, and then her skin was on his.

"I'm going to want to finish this, Danica…."

"Because all you care about right now is how I'm making you feel." Glancing down longingly at his stiff flesh, she gave another few strokes before releasing him. "That's called *distraction,* Dex, and it's a dangerous thing."

Righting his pants was no easy feat. Managing it, he

said, "Anything to prove a point, huh? Then show me you can be distracted. Show me I have an effect on you."

Steadily, carefully, he brought a hand to her outstretched leg and firmly stroked her from hip to thigh.

"Get your glass. Take a drink," he advised, his gaze not straying from her as she brought the cocktail to her lips.

"Now what?"

"Stop calculating." Dex massaged the inside of her thigh, heard the tiny moan she made against her glass. His hand skated over the exact spot where he was craving to dive into her. "Drop the facades. When you're with me, I want you naked."

She hesitated, and he had his answer. It wouldn't happen, not tonight. This wasn't the time or place, and she wasn't ready.

But crossing lines, breaking rules, it was inevitable. Lust hunted them. God help them when it caught up.

"This is more than distraction, Danica. We're heading for something we can't take back later." He let her go, disconnecting himself from her heat. "I'm looking forward to it."

Chapter 8

Danica wanted to lock herself in the lounge's powder room and interrupt her best friend's honeymoon so Veda could talk her down. But she had to settle for pressing a wad of cool, damp paper towels to her fevered cheeks and neck. There went her meticulously applied bronzer, but she didn't care.

She'd do great to go back into the lounge, pay the tab and say a friendly good-night to Dex Harper without jumping on him like the horn dog she was. To get so carried away with the possibilities of what his hands, his body and that voice could do to her was absurd. Danica Blue didn't sit in dark corners with off-limits men, or fantasize about dumping a pink bag of sex goodies onto her bed and sharing them with a very off-limits man who had a bad reputation and a wicked mind that she *really* wanted to get more acquainted with. Because it wasn't proper.

Proper was strolling down the aisle to Marion Reeves,

who'd looked stellar on paper. *Proper* was getting all tangled up in polo golden boy Ollie Johan, who had seemed so refreshing compared to the men who were too intimidated by her to even approach her. *Proper* was letting both Marion and Ollie lead her, when she was more than ready to make her own moves.

Sometimes being proper blew.

That didn't mean she would throw her sensibilities to the wind for Dex. She lost control, lost herself, when she was with him. Imperfections such as her occasional clumsiness, weakness for sweets and habit of analyzing the actual hell out of everything glowed like a flicker in a lantern whenever he got too close. Strangely, he hadn't walked away. In fact, he'd said he was "looking forward" to being with her.

Right. Until he sampled her and then sought out yet another actress or model or sports groupie. Marion had put in years of faithfulness, but eventually even he'd found satisfaction in other women's beds. Ollie had wooed her for weeks before accusing her of driving him out of her life with distrust, and she'd let him go. How long would it take Dex to move on? Was her curiosity morbid enough to compel her to find out?

She could do the safe thing—spare them both the awkwardness of going too far and regretting it.

Danica tossed the paper towels in the trash and reentered the lounge to find Dex gone and her shot and cocktail already paid for.

"This note was left for you." The bartender handed her a folded napkin.

"'Sir Galahad would never let a lady pay for his tequila, or her own.'"

With a smile, she slipped the note into her purse and

left the Luxor. Yes, she could do the safe thing. Or…she could take a risk.

She was itching to shake loose the stress that dug into her. She had hours of contract-loophole searching ahead of her, but diluting the potent energy that practically hummed inside her would do her a world of good. What she wanted was to laugh, gossip, dance.

Partying it up at the Marquee Nightclub at the Cosmopolitan with Lilith was as good a start as any. On a Saturday night, the line would be ridiculous, and Danica would have to flirt her way into the Marquee. But getting in to the main floor would be slightly less of a hassle on a Wednesday. It also helped that Lilith's cousin was on security.

The Marquee's line wrapped around the building. Despite the daytime heat, autumn whispered in the air at night.

Danica hoofed it toward the end of the line, knowing she'd regret walking all the way back *and* tackling the club's infamous stairs. Midway through the trek, a pair of clean-shaven men who'd recognized her as Temperance Blue's daughter waved her down and offered her a cut.

Careful not to disturb the man in front of them, who was in sagging jeans, smelled like weed and was cussing viciously into his Bluetooth, she indulged in a few moments of conversation with the men who'd let her jack the line. One was a real-estate agent; his partner was a photographer who knew her mother through mutual friends.

"You are retro Tem, but with a little spice," he praised. "Too damn sexy to be going solo at the Marquee."

"I'm meeting a friend." She craned her neck, but the effort was futile since even exotic-looking half Indonesian, half African-American Lilith was as difficult to spot in this crowd as Waldo on a wall mural.

"Good for you. Not my business to say this, but there

are parents out there—who shall remain nameless—who think having single adult children is as terrible as anything." He gave her a wink, but she'd have to be missing her brain to not know that her own mother was one of those *nameless* parents.

Not in the mood to wait for hours, Danica dialed her assistant's cell number. "Can't see you, Lil. I swear this line circles the building twice."

"Start by getting out of line," Lilith said, her voice nearly buried under the crushing bass. "I'm at the door with security."

Sure enough, when Danica made her way to the entrance, she saw her waiflike assistant squeezed between two beefy men—both with tats and one with a good two feet of beard. All in the space of a few minutes, Lilith led her through the dark, sexy interior of the club, scored them free margaritas and glow sticks, passed on a group of men's offer to relinquish their thousand-dollar bottle-service table and all but dragged Danica to a prime spot on the dance floor.

"This DJ is *insane!* What's better than a badass DJ?" Lilith swayed and dipped and gyrated to the music, while Danica considered the question.

"Hot apple cider."

"What?" Lilith's eyes narrowed under her ruler-straight black bangs, showing downright confusion.

"You asked what's better," Danica said, raising her voice. "There's an answer. Apple cider, cinnamon sticks, pumpkin pie. Some folks get spring fever. I get autumn fever."

"Oh!" Lilith managed to twirl around on the shoulder-to-shoulder dance floor, bumping her playfully. "That's what it is. I thought you were just crazy-hungry. Was two seconds away from suggesting you let one of those drooling dudes back at the table hook you up with a burger or something. Snap out of it, though, boss. My parents' new vacation house is in New Hampshire, and trust me, fall is the real thing there. Nothing Vegas can imitate. All the cider and cinnamon in the world won't change that."

When Lilith was right, she was right. Without dispute, Danica gave herself up to the music, letting the beat work its way into her bones as she danced—first with a few guys who weren't obsessed with patting her ass, then with Lilith, who persistently asked for her thoughts on a slew of men. "What about that guy over there? He's sort of short, but he's taller than you." "Do you think this one's attractive?" "How do you feel about Fu Manchu mustaches?"

"Not a fan of the Fu Manchu…but, Lil, my opinion doesn't carry a lot of weight. That's *your* potential man candy."

"'Man candy'?"

Suddenly, a man burst through the crowd and stood in front of them.

Oh, what fresh hell is this? Danica leveled an arch smile at Marion and braced herself.

"You corrupting my ex?" he said, drawing Lilith's hand to his lips. Always the man with the moves. He wore a pair of tinted glasses and dazzling bling on his fingers to complement his white designer ensemble.

"Trying to." Lilith's words, delivered in a monotone, were sassy and direct.

"Lil, this is my ex-husband, Marion. Marion, meet my assistant, Lilith Laurence." Danica then asked him, "And who are you here with?"

"The usual suspects," he said, referring to his entourage of friends, whose combined net worth could buy Las Vegas. As was commonly the case, he and his boys were likely painting Sin City in a procession of lowriders and luxury SUVs, with hulking bodyguards and paparazzi struggling to keep up. He took her hands. "Dance with me. Can't let a good song go to waste."

The DJ was digging up hits of the past, and the song shaking up the dance floor now was one of her favorites. Confetti burst from overhead, spiraling over the crush. It dotted people's hair, stuck to their heated skin, littered the dance floor.

Danica brushed the shimmering bits from her shoulders. "There's this thing that people say, Marion. 'Distance makes the heart grow fonder.'"

"Are you saying you want distance? All I did was cross your path and speak—out of respect to you."

"Thanks. But as for the dance? C'mon, seriously?"

"Yeah, we wouldn't want one dance to get in the way of you picking up a man. So, who is he?" Marion put his arms out, showing off his wingspan, and turned. As he did, people around them shuffled backward to give him the space he demanded.

"Marion, there isn't anyone—"

"You got on my case about honesty. Don't be a hypocrite now. Just point out the man who did this." Marion lifted her arm and stared at the scrawling signature on her skin. When she paused—torn between her initial instinct to tell him to take his sense of entitlement to hell and her second instinct to simply ignore him—Marion whipped around to her assistant. "Know who did this?"

Lilith spied the ink, and her eyes narrowed as recognition dawned. But she apparently had no qualms about lying. "Nope."

"Is this a tat, Danni?"

"No." Danica shook free, thinking quickly of how to diffuse the situation with hundreds watching. "Got a table,

Marion? If talking like civilized grown-ass adults is cool
with you, then let's do it there."

Marion led the way, and when his friends relinquished
the table to offer the most privacy anyone could get at the
Marquee, she asked, "Where's this possessiveness coming from?"

He exhaled, putting his hands together and bowing his
head. "All right. I meant no disrespect."

"Getting in my face, acting like you own me, seems
pretty disrespectful. Life isn't a reality TV show, Marion,
and it'd be productive for us both if you'd remember that
before stirring up drama in the middle of a club."

"What if I wanted you back?"

That was laughable, considering they both knew that
in his heart of hearts he didn't. "You had me, Marion, and
got tired of me. We didn't fight. We didn't compete against
each other. We were friends."

"Friendship's not enough to make a marriage stick."

"Nothing I gave you was enough. I tried to be *everything* you wanted, without ever asking you to change for
me. But that doesn't even matter anymore. It's better this
way—to be apart. Now that I've accepted that, the hurt
can stop. 'Cause I don't want this. I want something more."

Lilith sidled up to the table with a probing "Everything okay?"

"Just apologizing to Danni," Marion said.

"Apologize to Lilith."

Marion gave Danica a final repentant look before he
addressed her assistant. "Forgive me. Danni can put you
in touch with my secretary. She'll set you up with two
tickets to Fight Night. Car, too." Then he left them alone
at the table.

Danica should've been relieved at his absence, but she
felt unsettled. Wary. Confused. "Marion and I would never

be mistaken as a poster couple for happy endings, but that was strange. In his defense, though, he never had a crappy temperament when we were married. Always a jokester."

"He certainly strives to leave an impression. Know how much those tickets are worth? And am I right to assume that by 'car,' he means limo?"

"'Go all out or don't go at all' should be his motto. That offer is from him to you, Lil, so don't you dare feel you're a traitor to accept it."

Lilith grinned. "My boyfriend loves boxing more than he loves me, computers and his eighteen-year-old dog combined. He wouldn't want me to pass this up."

Boyfriend? "You're still with the IT guy? I thought you might've broken up. So why the man-hunting?"

Lilith was toying with her glow bracelet, but now she stilled. "For you."

"You were considering Fu Manchu for *me?*"

"I thought you could use a night out. You're so lone—"

"For the love of all that's good and holy, don't say 'lonely.' I'm not *lonely.* I'm busy, with responsibilities. With work, in fact!" Danica had to consciously lower her voice, but humiliation rattled her. If she'd only known that this night of barhopping and man-hunting was just Lilith's charity, then…what?

Her thoughts scrolled back to the Luxor and those naughty moments with Dex. His fingers had felt so good on her body, and if she hadn't had more pressing priorities keeping her in line, she might've simply let go.

And then where would she be? Chances were, she'd be with him. Which didn't sound like an altogether awful thing.

"I've offended you. Sorry, Danica."

"Don't give it another thought," she said with a crispness that wasn't totally directed at Lilith. Her assistant hadn't meant any harm, and she wasn't at the root of the turmoil that was festering within Danica.

Change was in the air—big-time—and it had nothing to do with the seasons.

"The work that needs to be taken care of? I can help."

"Thanks, but no." Danica swept up her purse, no longer in a clubbing mood. "I can do it alone."

She was more used to doing things alone than anyone around her realized. And holding that secret was one thing she *did* want to change.

Marion took to the Strip. He'd indulge in a game of blackjack, a gourmet meal and, if the mood struck him, a good-looking lady. But he was distracted by the ache for peace and quiet—the kind he could only get enclosed in his tinted-window car with his phone off.

Marion wore his every flaw with pride. Why shouldn't he? He'd earned the right to luxury, ruthlessness and self-indulgence. The years of learning what it took to survive in the insincere—no, cutthroat—entertainment world had sculpted him. He was arrogant, off-putting, an unapologetic flirt—he owned all that. Yet he took no pleasure in stepping to Danica the way he had done, putting on a show for a mass of intoxicated onlookers.

Getting her all insulted and defensive had cornered her to the point that she had come back swinging. In spite of the nosedive the night had taken, he'd left the Cosmopolitan with an important piece of information: Danica was different. Not just in appearance. Those leather pants and that ink covering the inside of her arm like a tattoo had thrown him off, but something else had changed.

I want something more.

She had meant it. What she'd said, the writing on her arm—it was driving him crazy that he'd been unable to make out the signature—was falling into place. A realization slammed him as he swung his car into the parking lot of the low-key bar he went to when he wanted privacy.

Danica had another man in her life.

As he settled down at his usual table for a late-night brandy, he took out his phone. When the call connected, he was greeted with a groggy curse that might've felt threatening if he wasn't at his boiling point. "Wake up. We need to get a few things straight," he returned, unaffected. Another vile oath. "There's a distinction between respect and politeness. My respect you've got with a lifetime guarantee. But lately you haven't exactly been earning the privilege of my politeness. Let's talk."

The conversation was brief, terse. At the end of it, he set his phone on the scratched wood table and sat back, finishing his brandy with a hard swallow.

Someone was getting to Danica. The mere fact that she wouldn't give him a name bothered him more than it should. Forthcoming, sweet, eager to please—that was his Danica.

"She's not mine anymore."

Chapter 9

NFL inquiries. Grueling interviews with a parade of investigators facing him down like a firing squad. Living caught in the grip of being viewed as a criminal. None of it was as brutal as silence. The silence had all but wrecked Dex since his big interview over a week ago. At Danica's urging, he'd taken his Corvette on a solo road trip to Burbank, California, to tape an exclusive talk-show interview. Danica had put him in direct contact with the host, advising that he get himself in front of a sympathetic audience. What he would say, what facets of himself he would share with the audience, was solely up to him.

"This is your game changer," Danica had insisted. "It's your play. Run it."

Dex had walked onto the set with every intention of being conversational and engaging—but even he knew that he'd come off as reticent and self-justifying. Over and over again, he'd deflected the host's attempts to unlock his past. She hadn't been malicious—in fact, she was witty and brash and funny as hell—but her questions had scratched the surface of his childhood and the person he most wanted to shield from his current life. The damage to his career and reputation had already managed to touch his younger sister, even though he never associated himself with Gunner, Oregon.

People in that town remembered him, and Erin talked too much for her own good. Still, she was better off there than with him.

After discussing the ongoing investigation, the host had set aside her note cards, leaned back in her chair and said, "Dex, last season the league fined you a hundred and fifty grand for punching your own teammate on the sidelines. What the fuck happened?" A gasp had rippled over the audience, and she'd promised cookies to her producers who would scramble to bleep the expletive.

"I sent a pass down the field with precision," Dex had explained. "I didn't overthrow the ball, but it looked that way because the receiver intentionally hesitated at a critical moment. I wasn't happy about it, he bumped me with his shoulder and I hit him. Gut reaction. I could've—probably *should've*—walked away, but I felt something was off. And I was right. Watch the clip again, listen closely to the audio and you'll hear something new. After I threw the punch and we were both being hauled to the tunnel, the receiver pointed to his jaw and said to Alessandro Franco, 'This is going to be extra.'"

After that, the dynamic of the interview had shifted, and he'd known that the truth had finally begun to hit home.

In the eight days that followed, he'd been met with nothing but silence. No word from his attorney, because nothing had changed. No update from his agent, either. Not even a text from Danica, who was likely waiting for the episode to air, waiting to see for herself whether he'd pissed on the opportunity she'd offered.

The stretch of quiet smothered him with a profound sense of aloneness. All of the unknowns surfaced—as did the sad reality that in this uncertain darkness he had no one but himself to count on.

He didn't know if working with Danica Blue in this last-ditch effort would pan out…didn't know if she'd offer up a pretty smile and walk away if the damage to his professional future proved too deep. Hell, he didn't know what she'd do if this half-baked plan to manipulate him into the hearts of the press and the public actually worked. Would she just congratulate herself on a pet project well done and walk away anyway?

Dex hated that the thought of her marching out of his life disturbed him. He couldn't stand that she was beginning to get to him on a level that was deeper than he wanted to recognize. He detested that eight days of silence between them could weaken him to the point that he didn't even want to find a random woman to distract him.

Then, once the episode had aired, she'd called him. And he'd lost his damn mind.

He'd just returned from the woodworking shed on his six-acre property. Exhausted, sweaty and ready to call it a night, he'd half listened to his voice-mail messages until he'd heard her voice—all honey and spice.

"Saw the interview," she'd said. "Can't get into it now, but I do have a couple of suggestions. I'll be admiring art all night at Great Exhibitions on the Strip, in case you're a glutton for my nitpicking."

His mind had stayed on Danica as he'd let the hot shower spray beat down on him. Staring through the water and steam, he'd worked the tension from his hot, hard flesh, imagining what they could do and be together if only it made sense. They each had every reason to seek someone without baggage and trouble. But maybe he couldn't quit surrounding himself with trouble, after all. And maybe she was drawn to it more than she wanted to accept.

Dex had been even more in tune with her when he'd arrived at Great Exhibitions, where he'd had absolutely no problem locating her. Wrapped tight in a short houndstooth-patterned dress and pointy-toed heels that could probably puncture a man's foot straight through, she was more fascinating than any painting or sculpture on display.

Once his gaze caught hers, she'd given him an impish smile. He'd followed her into a room that was vacant and dark, except for the filmy city lights penetrating the domed ceiling. Framed pieces of what he was pretty sure was impressionist art had lined the walls. White sheets had been draped over sculptures and more paintings, and the air smelled distinctly of clay and chemicals.

"It's been just hours since the show aired," Danica had said, hitching her purse strap over her shoulder, "and already networks—local and national—are getting swept up in the ripple effect. You handled yourself well, acted like a gentleman. I only suggest that if another golden nugget like this comes your way, you show the world that you weren't some lost boy who happened upon professional football. If your sister decides to cooperate with the press—"

"She won't."

"God, Dex. For such a hot-tempered and passionate man, you are unbelievably cold when it comes to your family." Even though she'd spoken softly, her words had seemed to echo through him. "Don't you even miss her?"

He'd given her a drawn-out beat of silence, and it'd felt briefly relieving to pass on that torturous feeling to someone else.

"Fine," she'd finally whispered when he reached for the door. There was the musical tattoo of her heels on the floor as she'd rushed up to him. "Then I have one last suggestion for you."

"What?"

Danica slipped into the space between his body and the exit, blocking him. "Miss me."

He'd sworn to himself that he wouldn't get drawn into touching her, or being the first to make contact tonight. "Danica, I miss you in ways a good girl like you might not want to hear."

"I may be small, but I'm not fragile or afraid. Words are only words. They don't shock me."

"Which is what you want—to be shocked." Dex had betrayed himself by touching her anyway, lifting her wrists between their bodies. "I miss you when I'm hard and ready, and I wish your hands were on me instead of mine. But those are only words, right?"

He'd guided her hands—not to his body, but her own. Cupping Danica's palms over her breasts, urging her to squeeze her flesh and moan in answer to the pressure, he'd muttered, "Miss me, Danica. Imagine every explicit, dirty move I can make on your body, and know that I can take it further."

In unspoken invitation, she had parted her legs, and he'd stepped between them, bringing his knee forward. All it had taken was a bend of her legs before she'd straddled him. Her eyes fixed on his, she'd ridden him, rocking herself against him as he worked her hands on her breasts.

"Know that you and I are greedy, selfish people, and sex might not be enough. Then realize that I'm not within reach, and maybe—*maybe*, Danica—you'll understand my hell."

Danica's orgasm had her writhing, trying to back away

from the sensation as she bit down on her lip to stifle a moan. In answer he'd maintained contact, had pressed his knee against the heat between her thighs, and she'd cried out his name in a voice that had sent a new degree of want unfurling through him.

But, satisfied that she'd gotten a taste of the fire they could ignite in each other, he'd released her hands, moved her aside and left the gallery. She had made the rules between them, and it was up to her to break them.

Now, not even forty-eight hours later, as Dex and his legal team wrapped up a videoconference with ESPN in Bristol, he was regretting that she wasn't with him. This morning the NFL had finally issued an official statement confirming that he was no longer under investigation for being on the take. Since his talk-show interview, web clips of the in-game misconduct incident had seen a substantial boost in views. ESPN had gotten hold of his attorneys this morning, and by sundown he'd found himself besieged with interview requests.

In the polished lobby of Washington, Yozeman & Birch, while Dex waited for the building's valet to bring his car, he checked his phone. Two text messages. One from his sister, Erin.

I ALWAYS HAD FAITH IN YOU. GET IN TOUCH. XOXO.

And one from Danica.

CONGRATS. THE LEAGUE GOT OFF ITS ASS. IT'S NOT OVER YET. ONWARD.

Dex didn't respond to either message. As Danica reminded him, the war wasn't over. All he'd done was establish that he hadn't been a dirty player. Yet the media still buzzed with speculation that his quarterback skills had gone to hell, and his reputation was a long way from repaired. Especially since it hadn't been golden to begin with.

That had been his own doing. He'd swaggered into the NFL with a chip on his shoulder and taken for granted the privileged lifestyle football had lent him. He hadn't let himself cope with leaving Oregon and losing both parents on his way to success. All that change might've made him crazy. Pretending not to be affected, as if nothing could get to the heart of him, had gotten him through. But a broken heart could overrule a rational mind any day.

In a suit and tie, Dex was already presentable enough to make an appearance at the Bellagio's Prime Steakhouse where his agent, Shaw Bordeaux, and his wife were treating their daughter and her twenty or so "closest" friends to a damn expensive dinner and a Fountains of Bellagio show in celebration of Sally Bordeaux's seventh birthday. He'd given his agent his word that he'd stick around to talk business—in spite of the fact that the thought of a swarm of hyper second-grade girls sparked the beginnings of a headache.

Shaw had been his agent since Dex's sophomore season in the NFL. He knew his shit and—though he was a cynical, glass-half-empty type—he'd never turned his back on Dex in the wake of all the trouble he'd landed himself in over the years. Even jobless, he still had Shaw in his corner, as an agent and a friend.

Armed with a porcelain doll, Dex stepped into the restaurant to be immediately bombarded by sticky-fingered little girls in party hats and frilly dresses.

"What'd you get her?"

"Lemme see!"

"*I'm* Sally's best friend. Let *me* see first!"

Shaw and his wife, Ramona, hustled forward to steer the mob of kids to their four-star meals at the elaborately decorated tables, but the girls squirmed free, mulishly hanging around as Sally flew to him with her hickory curls bouncing and a gap-toothed grin dominating her freckled face.

"Uncle Dex, you're here! I knew you'd come. Mommy said all of Daddy's friends are un-re-liable…. Did I get the word right, Mommy?"

Ramona cleared her throat. "Well enough, Sally. Dex, can I get you a glass of champagne from the bar?"

"Ramona Bordeaux, that's the closest you've ever come to apologizing to me. I'll take that champagne before you change your mind."

"Wise decision." But she was smiling as she lightly socked his shoulder.

Sally was staring intently at the pink-wrapped package under his arm. "Is that a present for me?" Batting those big green eyes, the kid all but melted his heart. Amazingly, in spite of what he'd been through and who he'd become, he still had a heart capable of melting.

Dex handed her the gift. "Of course it is, Mustang Sally."

She beamed at the nickname he'd given her when she was still in diapers, testing her father's patience every time Shaw had been forced to merge his duties as a father and a sports agent and had let her tag along with him to work.

Tearing at the gift wrap and jetting off like a pale pink cyclone, Sally showed off the doll to her friends and left him to pick up the scraps of colorful paper and ribbons.

Shaw greeted him and led the way to a table cluttered with dinnerware but free of cake frosting stains and freakish-looking balloon animals. Grown-ups' table. Hallelujah.

"I'm starting to think that nickname's having a self-fulfilling prophecy effect," Shaw said.

"What, is she changing too fast for you and Ramona to keep up?" Dex took a seat and a moment later Ramona was there with his champagne before she stomped off again to tend to the distinct screeching sounds of little girls yelling at each other.

"Hell, yes. It makes me worry about the future. Me, in my fifties, trying to keep up with a teenager? Won't be pretty." Shaw chuckled, then, sobering, said, "So, ESPN made contact. All that means is they want information on the investigation and have figured out that you're the best shot they have at getting it."

"What does that mean for me?"

"Nothing concrete. A hope that one of the franchises will grow a pair—" Catching himself, Shaw cleared his throat. "A hope that now a franchise will be forward-thinking enough to sign you up. Three weeks are going to go by effin' fast, Dex. If we're going to get you on a roster, we'd need to get you in serious talks this week. I have a list of ball clubs with weak offenses."

Ramona plopped down onto the chair between them. "Dex, you had yourself a bit of a victory today, so I'm not going to ream you boys out for leaping into football mode in the middle of my only child's birthday party." She leaned and kissed Shaw on the lips. "But I *will* ask you to take the conversation outside."

"Fair enough," her husband said.

"And, Dex," she added, getting up. "Not that I'm rushing to make myself president of your fan club, but I didn't think that even a hellion like you had turned dirty."

Dex contemplated that while he downed the rest of his champagne. The moment he'd been released from the team, he swore he was in this fight alone. Getting the crap kicked out of him when he'd moved to Louisiana as a teenager had taught him to fight alone—for survival. Yet the suspicion and jadedness were starting to chip away, unveiling truths that might always have existed but he hadn't been inclined to see.

Setting aside his glass, he saw his agent frown and then was aware of a trail of kids skipping toward their table, as if in a bizarre conga line, with Sally at the front.

"Um, I have a question," she announced, glancing behind her at the giggling girls.

"I'll give you and your dad some privacy, then."

Dex started to get up, but Sally stopped him with a shrill "Wait!"

Shaw pinched the bridge of his nose. "Indoor voice, Sally."

"But you yell on the phone all the time."

"Yeah, well, this is one of those 'do as I say, not as I do' cases. What's your question?"

"It's not for you, Daddy." Sally twirled a curl around her finger. "Uncle Dex, since I have a new party dress and you love me and I love you…um, how about we have a wedding today?"

Damn, he was *not* expecting this. Dex looked to Shaw for assistance, but the man had averted his face and his shoulders were shaking with piss-poorly contained laughter. To make it worse, the few grown-ups who'd overheard the girl's proposal were gushing, "Awww!"

Sally's face was so hopeful that even Dex couldn't justify walking away without setting her straight. "I appreciate that you love me, Sally," he said carefully, keeping her fragile, impressionable young heart in mind. "But we're friends, and the friendship kind of love is different from the marriage kind. Plus, you're not old enough to marry anyone."

The other girls groaned with disappointment. Then

Sally protested, "Today's my birthday. I'm seven. Mommy bought me roses 'cause I'm a big girl now."

"Right. But you're still a child. I'm an adult. Adults marry adults. So how about we stay friends, just as we are? That okay with you, birthday girl?"

Sally slowly nodded. "Okay." Then she and her friends hurried from the table, and within a few short moments they were pigging out on cake, the marriage proposal as good as forgotten.

"A little help with that would've been friggin' great," Dex said to Shaw.

Shaw, whose complexion had turned ruddy during his laughing fit, took a fortifying breath as he shook his head. "A girl's first choice is always the bad boy, huh?" Seeing Dex's dark glower, he put up his hands in a surrendering gesture. "C'mon. I need a cigarette. After what just happened, I bet you wish you were a smoking man, too."

Dex had more than his share of vices, but smoking had never appealed to him. He waited while Shaw lit a cigarette on the garden patio.

"That talk-show interview," Shaw said. "The Slayers' GM orchestrated that. She's been whispering in your ear for a couple of weeks now, and as genuine as she might seem, she *is* Marshall and Temperance Blue's errand girl. I've got to wonder if this is more of a business tactic than a Good Samaritan act. Corday looked good on Monday night, but he's had a shaky start with that shoulder. Kip Claussen says he's got confidence in their backup QBs. What if that's all talk, though?"

"Shaw, I'm not going back to that mentality. The deal is Danica helps me sign with another team this season and I don't come knocking on the Slayers' door asking for my job back." Except it was more textured, more complex than that.

"Just because you're no longer being investigated doesn't mean you're going to get an offer. A cynic asshole's born every minute. Spoken from the best of the breed. As good as you are, you've got baggage. Organizations don't want that. You can talk to the media from sunup to sundown, but you'll be spinning your wheels. Show the NFL that you're a new man. A man committed to the American dream."

Shaw looked at him through a haze of smoke. "Why not try the family plan and get yourself married? Ever heard of Tiffany Wilder-Gardenshire? Her grandfather's an oil tycoon, and she's one of the country's top philanthropists under thirty. Cancer research, church funding, environmental rescues—she's all up in it. Get a woman like that to wear your ring, show the world that you're the settling-down type, and you'll see results faster than you would doing anything else. A connection between the NFL and the Gardenshires would be a win for the league and for you."

"What the hell are you really smoking?"

"Ha. Ha. Ha," Shaw said dryly. "There are worse things than getting hitched, and worse reasons to do it than for financial or social gain."

"Is that your and Ramona's story?"

"Karma must've been on my side the day I met Ramona. I don't deserve her, and I worry that one of these days she's gonna have that epiphany. But until then, I'm a happy man." Shaw cracked his neck. "Dex, all I'm trying to show you is a possibility that might work out. Marrying Tiffany, or someone with similar connections, can resuscitate your reputation. Marriage is just like any other business. It needs to make sense. Love and all that—it's kid stuff. Inconsequential."

"Afraid I don't see it that way, Shaw. Not everything in this life is *just business*."

"Careful, Dex. Your small-town values are showing."

"I can thank my lucky effin' stars for the few values I have left."

Shaw didn't push the issue further, only disposed of his cigarette and shook his head the way he did whenever he thought something was a damn shame.

His wife poked her head outside, scrunching up her face at the residual fingers of smoke fading into the air. "Babe, we'd all better start herding the kids outside if we don't want to miss the last show."

"Then let's go." Shaw gave Ramona's rear a light clap and guided her inside.

Dex followed, cutting a quick path through the restaurant. He'd almost reached the exit when Ramona called after him, "Won't you be joining us for the show?"

Just when he thought he was free...

As always, Danica was early. She was having dinner at the Bellagio with her mother and Veda's mother, Willa, at seven sharp. When it came to the ladies' appetite for gossip, Danica's foresight was 20/20. She could all but visualize them left alone at a table, indulging in wine and small talk about Willa's recently married daughter, who'd be returning from her honeymoon in a few days. Naturally, the chat would shift to what pointers the expert Willa could offer to Tem's three *un*married daughters, starting with the one they'd be dining with tonight.

So Danica had taken extraspecial care to park at the Bellagio at six. That gave her a one-hour cushion to gamble at the casino, tour the hotel, twiddle her thumbs or find a quiet little nook to relax and silence the restlessness that was setting her on edge.

On a whim she set her sights on the lake walkway, eager to check out the fountains show's new repertoire.

A tepid October breeze tickled her legs as she walked in her cream high-necked swing dress toward the assembly of onlookers outside the casino. The magic had already begun. Glittering spurts of water shot up from the man-made lake, in time with a classic Broadway tune.

"Lady, I can't see."

Danica looked down at the tiny finger prodding her hip. A girl in a ruffled dress stared up at her, saucerlike brown eyes fluttering.

"Uh, where are your parents?"

"Pearl, you're not supposed to talk to strangers!" Another girl, this one in a pale pink bubble dress and shiny Mary Jane pumps, wiggled between them. "We're supposed to stick together, 'cause that's how the buddy system works. I'm going to tell my parents you're not following the rules, and they'll tell your mom—"

Danica crouched down, interrupting with, "Where are *your* parents, then?"

"Kissing," Pearl supplied in a singsong voice. "So there!"

"Are not!"

"Are, too. My sister said lots of grown-ups come here and watch the water show and it's romantic and they smooch. Oooohhhh." Pearl smirked. "Sally's parents, sitting in a tree. K-I-S-S-I-N-G!"

Sally thumped her buddy's arm, drawing a sharp yelp. "They're not in a tree. They're standing over there."

Danica looked to the group. Over a dozen more little girls stood in pairs, with a handful of adult chaperones. All seemed captivated by the show.

No one was kissing, though it was apparent that the man and woman snuggled close belonged to Sally. When the man turned his face to say something to the woman, Danica recognized him.

"Sally, is your last name Bordeaux?"

"Yes." The way her delicate eyebrows rose over a pair of green eyes conveyed, *What's it to you?*

"I've met your father." As if the initial tense meeting with Shaw, when she'd officially released his star client from the team's roster, hadn't gotten them off to a rocky start, he'd recently visited her office to dissuade her from "being an enabler" and puffing Dex up with delusions about his career prospects. Emotion had made her sloppy, though, and she'd fired off a rant that revealed she was more invested in Dex's future than an ex-employer ought to be.

"She's met me, too," a man said.

Danica wanted to thump herself for reacting to Dex's voice with a full-body shiver. He winked at her, and despite the articulate greeting her brain had woven, all that came out was an unintelligible, strangled noise that sounded like "Hooo."

The kids flocked to him, Sally tattling, "Pearl snuck off, Uncle Dex. She didn't follow the rules."

"Sally thumped me!"

"Apologize," he said. "Tell each other why you're sorry, shake hands and move on."

Grumbling, "Okay," the girls faced each other.

"Sorry I broke the buddy system rules," Pearl said. "Oh, and for singing the kissing song about your parents."

"Sorry I thumped you," Sally replied, putting out her hand, which her friend shook with an infectious laugh.

"I only snuck off because I couldn't see the water," Pearl insisted to Dex. "I was asking this lady for help. Who is she?"

"This is my friend Danica," he said. "Let's get you two hooligans back to the group. And this time, stay put."

A smile worked its way to Danica's mouth as she

watched him escort the girls to the rest of their party. The man was emotionally orphaned, had gone years without family connections, yet his heart wasn't as cold as people—including him, she'd bet—assumed.

He'd make an incredible father.

It startled her that the thought could flood her with hope.

In another few minutes he was in front of her again, and her heart was bouncing in her chest. "What's up, *friend?*"

"The lady speaks," he said with a teasing grin. "What was that strange injured-owl noise you made?"

"I was choking." *On lust.* "How'd you wind up chaperoning a pack of kids?"

"It's Sally Bordeaux's birthday. If I'd thought you'd be out here, I would've smuggled you a slice of birthday cake. I know how much you enjoy cake."

Danica could swear the back of her neck tingled, as if that specific spot on her body possessed its own store of memories...such as Dex's mouth tasting her there. Even that had only been preparation for the pleasure he'd given her two nights ago at Great Exhibitions. Dry-humping in an art gallery... What *wouldn't* she do if she got this man alone again?

"I'm having dinner at Picasso, with a matchmaker." Watching him closely, she saw his jaw tighten, then release. What she'd said had gotten to him. It satisfied her when she knew it shouldn't. "The matchmaker is my best friend Veda's mother. My mom's joining us. Make no mistake— neither is pleased with my romantic track record—but I'm not on the prowl for a match."

Dex's gaze cruised her slowly. "How long have you been single?"

"Months."

"You've been alone every night since then?"

Danica moistened her lips. "Yes."

His knuckles brushed her from shoulder to elbow so swiftly she wasn't sure if she'd daydreamed it. "That's a damn tragedy."

"I get by." His eyes narrowed with intrigue, and the word *how* passed his lips. She scrambled to avoid answering. "So, you're a badass athlete, a chivalrous Sir Galahad type, a man who's more *con*structive than *de*structive and you're wonderful with kids. Churchill described something as 'a riddle wrapped in a mystery inside an enigma.' I'd say you fit that description."

"Then we have something in common." Dex came closer, and she felt a naughty thrill as his scent fell over her. "Guess you're finding out there's a lot about me you won't see in my file."

"I wish I could take my time discovering you," she whispered. "But we don't have the luxury of time. I'm on your side, if you haven't figured that out by now. Football is what's most important to you, and I'll do whatever I can to get you in the game. Next step is simply this. Let yourself be seen involved in a cause that people care about."

"Danica—"

"Dex, I know your secret. I know in here—" she tapped her index finger to her temple "—and here—" she tapped her heart "—that you're not a hard-hearted bastard." She stepped around him to start heading for Picasso. "Think of what *you* care about, and go there."

Danica walked away, and once she was within the safe confines of the restaurant, she fanned herself with her clutch purse.

"Danica, are you feeling all right?" Tem asked as she approached. She reached as though to press the back of her hand against her daughter's forehead, and Danica was about to smile at the tender gesture until she realized that

Tem was only attempting to smooth her windblown bangs. "Freshen up in the ladies' room, why don't you?"

Beside her, stately Willa Smart added, "We'll order you tea."

"I'm fine. I was just outside watching the fountain show." *I'm lying. I'm not fine. I'm about to claw out of my skin because I'm so hot for a man I can't have.*

"That wasn't very sensible. We'll have a lovely view of the lake right from our table." Tem gave Willa an exasperated look before she held Danica at arm's length for an inspection. Concern dimmed her usually vivid eyes as they paused on one arm then the other. Was she searching for something? "Always think sensibly, Danica."

Danica watched Tem greet the hostess with her perfect smile, perfect posture, perfect not-a-strand-out-of-place hairstyle. Never would she measure up to her mother. Continuing to try would only make her a wannabe Temperance Blue. But what was wrong with being an original Danica Blue?

Tem strode back to her. "Come to the table," she said under her breath. "You look like a lost puppy just standing here at the hostess's station. Men are staring as if they want to take you home."

Danica opened her purse, her ears hot and her palms damp. "Just have a call to make."

"Go, then. Want the tea or wine?"

"Wine." *A bottle ought to get me through this dinner....*

Danica chastised herself for the snide thought. "Thank you, Ma. Be right back." Tem was already sashaying off to join Willa.

Outside the restaurant, Danica dialed slowly, giving herself every opportunity to change her mind. If it rang three times with no answer, she'd hang up and let that be the end of it.

Dex answered on the first ring.

"That night at the art gallery…" Closing her eyes, she blocked out everything but the truth. "That night, in my bed…I missed you."

Danica hung up, not giving him a chance to get a word in edgewise. Let him untangle the undertones of what she'd said, the magnitude of what she was capable of wanting. Doing. Wanting to do again.

In the restaurant, Tem waved her over to sit at the empty seat next to her. "Why is it, Willa, that my girls insist on vexing me?" She finally turned to Danica. "I had assumed you'd take an opportunity to fix your hair or makeup, at least. Looking a little feral tonight."

"Oh." Danica picked up her wineglass. And smiled.

Feral. She liked the sound of that.

Chapter 10

Danica hadn't planned to skip work. The shrill beeping of Alarm Clock 1 woke her early on Saturday, and Alarm Clock 2 quickly joined in.

Her phone rested next to her tablet on the nightstand, along with a neglected bonsai tree and a heavy lamp, which she'd left glowing all through the night when she powered off the phone, tossed her stuff down and collapsed on the four-poster bed in a state of stress-induced exhaustion.

With last night's makeup smudging her pale sheets, and the day's list of to-do items funneling through her mind, she emerged from her burrow under the covers at the foot of the bed to stare bleary-eyed at the clocks.

Motivated by the challenge to dress and hurry her pa-tootie out the door on schedule, Danica showered, wrapped herself in a towel and, with her phone in tow, padded barefoot to her home office to coordinate her calendars.

But, leaning over her desk chair, confronted with calendars on the wall, on the desk, on her computer and her phone—square after square dictating where she was expected, dividing the precious moments of her life—she felt something inside her give way.

Dialing feverishly, she connected herself to the HR after-hours answering service. It wasn't in her contract to regularly report to the admin building on Saturdays, but she'd stumbled into the routine of haunting the place, whiling away the day in her office, sometimes surrounded by colleagues, other times alone. All because she'd rather be alone at the stadium than alone in this house.

For good measure, she texted her assistant.

UNAVAILABLE TODAY.

If necessary, Lilith, who almost never worked on Saturdays, would report directly to Marshall and Tem.

Not once since accepting the GM position had Danica made herself "unavailable." Doing so filled her with a strange rush of giddiness that she knew was only temporary and would come crashing down in a matter of time.

So until that time came, there was only Danica, and anyone else she let into her world. At six o'clock in the morning, there wasn't a minute to waste.

With a daring intake of breath, she flicked open her towel and let it fall to a terry cloth puddle at her feet. Naked, alone in her house with all its ghosts of memories that were quiet for now, she marched out of the office. Fixing an omelet and savoring each bite au naturel was paradise compared to her usually rushed muffin and coffee from Starbucks.

But as she ate standing at the counter with the television on mute, a plan pieced itself together in her thoughts. To start, she would get dressed, launder her bedding, meticulously dust the entire upstairs floor of the mansion—and get reacquainted with its interesting nooks and crannies along the way.

But she had gotten only as far as the dressing part, throwing on a sweatshirt over jeans, before she'd spontaneously decided to contact her home-security team.

Overseeing the gate reset nibbled the better part of an hour, and by the time the technician gave her a refresher walk-through of the security cameras' connections to the centralized computer, she'd been all but shaking with relief to sign job-completion papers, shake his hand and send him on his merry way.

Danica closed the front door behind the technician, then rested her forehead against the wood. No more of Marion Reeves getting past the gate…or her defenses. It was another ending, another piece of finality tumbling into place. But this time, wistfulness didn't take her by the shoulders and rattle her.

There were no tears. No hard feelings. Nothing but acceptance.

Treat yourself. Pushing away from the door and thundering upstairs in the palace of a house to ransack her walk-in for a change of clothes, Danica made a promise to herself that she'd do just that. "I'm going home."

Home was on East Poplar Avenue, snuggled between the city's housing authority and Hadland Park. Sprawled on a generous lot, garnished with professionally manicured grounds, Faith House's two-year-old main building rose three stories into the sky. Cast in sunlight, the front lawn's fountain glimmered even from the street. The youth-outreach center was a beacon, a lighthouse calling to the soft side of Danica's heart.

Tucking her Boxster between two trucks, she muscled

three paper bags stuffed with groceries from the car and greeted the doorman. "Morning, Mr. Hawkins."

"In all my days watchin' this door, I've never seen you here on a Saturday morning," he observed, allowing her into the lobby. "It sure is a nice treat."

"The treats are in here." She jiggled the bags as one of the volunteer tutors came forth to lighten the load. "I thought Raoul and I could offer the kids a baking lesson later. Cupcakes. A batch with the original recipe, and one that's low carb. Don't want to leave out anyone special."

Mr. Hawkins's face split into a smile. While most people Danica knew made demands as effortlessly as they blinked, Mr. Hawkins dependably worked his shifts without ever requesting anything, not a raise or an extra break or time off. Even something as everyday as a cupcake he wouldn't ask for, which was why Danica had kept the fifty-something diabetic gentleman in mind as she'd shopped for ingredients.

As president of Faith House, Danica often spent her visits to the center in the third-floor conference room, laboring over executive details with the board of directors. Grant proposals and fund-raisers were bumps in the rough terrain on her path to show Las Vegas's kids that a hard life on the streets didn't have to be their destiny. Danica knew from the PR and financial departments, as well as volunteer staff, that teens as young as thirteen years old walked through Faith House's doors in search of a hot meal, a person to listen, some possibility of escape from gangs, homelessness, drugs, prostitution and violence.

Rarely did Danica see those children's faces. Since agreeing to head up her parents' football team, she'd run the outreach center from a distance. It was a distance that she resented. She'd rather spend more time on the first and second floors, working side by side with the staff, volunteers and the people they were committed to rescuing.

In fractions of moments when Danica stopped to just take a breath, she'd think about the teen who had slinked into her life with the intent to cause her harm. Instead, Danica had saved her life—only to have it cut short, anyway.

When Faith Rivera, a sixteen-year-old dropout with a rap sheet, had died in an auto explosion, she'd been treated as a statistic. A blip in a news report of yet another Vegas degenerate youngster who'd met an early demise.

Until Danica had devoted herself to changing that. Now anyone who discovered Faith House would know the girl's story. They'd know Faith Rivera's life mattered.

After putting away the groceries in the center's industrial-style kitchen and charming Raoul, the cantankerous, set-in-his-ways chef, to let her invade his haven for a cupcake-baking extravaganza later, Danica dug right in wherever she was needed. The morning was spent assisting in tutoring sessions, and then she was tugged away to meet with one of the crisis-shelter execs, who'd gotten word of her presence at the chief building and insisted on meeting with her to iron out details about this year's holiday fund-raiser.

On her way out of the crisis shelter's executive building, she checked her cell.

Among a string of text messages from colleagues that all began with some variety of "I know you're not working today, *but...*" and voice mails from friends inviting her out for shopping or supper, was a text message from Dex.

STILL MISSING ME?

Danica stared at the phone until the display faded to black. Finally, she pushed through the doors of the exit and dialed his number. When he picked up, she swiped a hand over her abdomen, as if the motion would net the butterflies taking flight in her stomach. "Calling you the other night, telling you that I touched myself thinking about you, was a crazy impulse—"

"Figured you'd try to take us a step back," he murmured over the line. "Problem with that is, telling me or not telling me doesn't change that it's true."

"So, are you going to let me finish saying what I was going to say?"

"Yeah. Go ahead."

"I *shouldn't* have called you," she said, meandering to her car in the lot. The butterflies in her stomach had metamorphosed into a dangerous heat dipping low inside her, licking unforgivably at her flesh. "I should've told you to your face. Maybe even shown you."

Dex groaned a curse, and the filthy word all but thrilled the Goth-purple polish off her toes. "Danica…"

"That can still happen, Dex. But not now." She fished her key chain from her purse. "I'm chillin' at Faith House today. It's sanity that I've really been missing lately."

Ending the call and sliding behind the wheel of her Boxster, Danica sighed. She was free-falling, right into trouble. Should she trust Dex to catch her when she reached the bottom? And if he did, would she want him to ever let her go?

You and I are greedy, selfish people, and sex might not be enough.

Or would she only be setting herself up for another heartbreak?

She brushed that heap of complication from her thoughts like grains of sand and returned to the outreach center. The on-site counselors, tutors and a sprinkle of potential sponsors all competed for her attention.

The first real snag came when she and one of the kitchen volunteers rounded up the teens for a lesson in food prep.

"Cooking? As in, home ec? That shit—I mean, that *stuff*—is for females," a boy protested as the group trickled into the spacious dining room.

"Is that so?" a girl fired back. "Then I don't want to see your caveman ass eating a cupcake. You're just punkin' out 'cause for once you can't show off."

Danica intervened. "Gentlemen. Ladies. Cupcakes shouldn't be an emotionally charged subject. To be accurate, though, plenty of men are happy to cook—and extremely good at it."

The boy twisted his mouth in a "yeah, right" expression.

"Men like Emeril Lagasse and Guy Fieri," the volunteer put in.

"Naw, I'm talkin' about real-world dudes."

"Like me?" Raoul, in his signature do-rag, jeans and the khaki uniform shirt that was strikingly plain in contrast to the colorful abstract tattoos on his thickly muscled arms, held open the kitchen's double swinging doors.

Now, *there* was a "real-world dude," and if the boy's resigned sigh and sheepish look to his peers was anything to go by, he figured so, as well.

"Wash hands, everybody," Raoul, captain of the kitchen, commanded, "and let's get to it."

A benign lesson in cupcakes turned into a fiercely competitive bake-off. Danica couldn't have wished for a better result. Batches of creatively frosted cupcakes beautified the center's kitchen, before one by one the treats started disappearing as the kids rushed to eat their handiwork. No flaring tempers or injuries—just an entire pan of batter hitting the floor and decorating the shoes of the few teens standing close.

As five o'clock loomed, the demands began to thin.

Closing time was in another hour. Danica was passing the receptionist's desk when she heard Nellie shriek, "Oh, my freaking gosh!"

Approaching the desk, Danica looked through the glass interior doors toward the lobby...where Mr. Hawkins stood shaking hands with Dex Harper.

"Is he coming in?" Nellie asked hopefully, glancing at Danica. "I want an autograph for my sister. Wait—uh, don't the Slayers people consider him *persona non grata?*"

"There are no hard feelings. Why don't I see what I can do about getting you that autograph?"

Nellie nodded enthusiastically, but the ringing phone slapped her professionalism into place. "Good afternoon. Faith House." The crisp, attentive tone was a stark difference to the infatuated-girl-on-the-prowl shrieking of a few moments before.

Danica made it through the interior doors as Mr. Hawkins let Dex past the front entrance. They met in the middle of the atrium lobby. Fingers of late-afternoon sunlight penetrated the glass, streaking over his mussed hair and the shoulders of his simple yet exquisitely fitted dark shirt. In a romantic film, this would be the moment that they'd be wrapped up in each other. But since this was reality, and their reality included rules, expectations and, of course, security guards scrutinizing them behind opaque sunglasses, Dex shook her hand in the same fashion that he'd greeted the doorman.

The contact jolted her, calling to life a billion little sensations that danced with anticipation. "I'm beginning to think you enjoy catching me off guard," she whispered. "When I said that I'd be hanging out here today, it wasn't a roundabout way of asking you to come see me."

"Think about the place I care about and go there—that's what you told me at the Bellagio. I want to see the place *you* care about." His mouth—oh, sweet God, his beautiful mouth—quirked into a private smile. "And hell, yes, I like you off guard."

"What's with that hungry look in your eyes?"

"I'm off guard, too, Danica. I wasn't expecting you to smell like dessert."

And you'd devour me if I let you.... "We had a bake-off. Think *Cupcake Wars,* teen edition."

He smiled, and her heart karate-chopped her ribs. "C'mon in," she said, raising her voice for security's benefit. "The receptionist tells me that she'd like an autograph." She escorted him inside, where a flock of gawking teenagers were already stationed around Nellie's desk.

Danica stood a safe distance away from the mob of kids who were assailing Dex with praise for his athletic prowess and prying questions about the investigation. It wasn't every day that they met a professional athlete up close and personal. The group trip to a Slayers home game at the start of the season had been a onetime treat. Though she was the founder and president of Faith House, and the general manager of the Slayers, they were still two entirely separate entities.

"There's a football in the equipment locker," Kiefer, a boy with a pierced eyebrow and impressive cupcake-frosting techniques, said. A victim of physical abuse, he'd come to the center as a reserved, quiet boy, but now he was settled in a new foster home and more outspoken. "Can you give us some pointers?"

"Outside," Nellie added, appearing a bit concerned at the thought of an indoor scrimmage.

"I'm always ready for football," Dex said. Competing with the raucous cheers, he hollered to Danica, "What about you? Want to get in on this?"

"Not in these shoes." Valentino slim-heeled pumps

weren't made for loping in the grass. Neither were the tuxedo-style blazer and calf-length trousers she'd spiced up with Goth-inspired jewelry, smoky makeup and a sheer pink blouse with a black bow collar.

Danica designated herself cheerleader on the makeshift sidelines while the others lost themselves in practicing passes. The hour rolled much too soon, and she was sorry to see Nellie trek out to announce closing time.

"I wish I could freeze this day, hang on to it, you know?" she confided in Nellie as the two brought up the rear of the group.

The receptionist nudged her companionably. "You'll just have to come by more often. Will we see you at the free brunch the crisis center's hosting? Oh, no, no. Football time, isn't it? Big game tomorrow."

"If only I could add a few more days to the week, hmm."

Nellie smiled, subtly pointing to Dex. "He was a nice surprise. Did you put him up to dropping in?"

"No, that was all on him. He's exactly that. A surprise. Preconceptions, they trip us up."

"Whoa, that's heavy. What do you mean?"

Danica spied Dex up ahead, handing the football to Kiefer, who jogged ahead to the main building. "Take Dex. Before I met him I was sure I had him pegged. He's more than his nickname and his reputation. He's…a nice guy."

"I'll say. To come here and play football with a bunch of kids on his birthday. If that's not the mark of a 'nice guy,' then—"

"Rewind." Danica stopped Nellie with a light grip on her wrist. "*Today* is his birthday?"

"Google seems to think so. When y'all headed out here, I called my sister to tell her about his visit, and she nearly punctured my eardrum with this cray-cray girl-meets-boy-band scream. She insisted that today's his B-day, and I looked up his bio on the internet."

Danica met Dex's eyes as she and Nellie stepped inside. In unspoken agreement he waited while the kids, then Raoul, then Nellie left. The cleaning crew had arrived and was flipping on lights until the entire main floor glowed. Outside, the sky was darkening into a wash of deep reds and purples as daylight wilted.

Once she'd retrieved her dessert—the neatly packed cupcake she'd decorated with a poor attempt at a calligraphy *D*—from the kitchen, she joined Dex at the reception desk.

"A 'happy birthday' is in order. Guess you're going to celebrate Vegas-style?"

"No plans."

"Shut. Up." Danica shook her head. "I mean, how can that be?"

"It's not that. I'm more selective about who I roll with these days. Fair-weather friends serve a purpose, but it's not to have my back. Real friends don't take off when shit hits the fan. My boy Russo's got an away game tomorrow, Shaw and his wife are still decompressing from their daughter's birthday, the Samuel Adams Utopias from Samantha already arrived…and I'm with you now."

She made the cut? The instant satisfaction was just as quickly doused with guilt. It was ironic that his birth date slipped her mind when she could recall so many minute details of his employee file—such as he was a chess player and had completed light community service for speeding when he was at LSU. "I ought to tell you, then, that I forgot your birthday. Nellie clued me in."

"You're on my side, Danica. The rest isn't important."

"Your birthday *is* important. That sexy, cavalier grin thing isn't going to change my mind. Birthdays are miracles. They shouldn't be forgotten or ignored. They should be shared with people who care about you." She lifted the container. "I was going to save this for after dinner, but… um, I'd rather share it with you, Dex. The cupcake and your birthday."

Danica had a talent for saying things without actually saying them. Tonight she'd insisted that his birthday should be shared with someone who cared about him—and then nominated herself. If she cared, he wanted her to strip away the games and just say so.

She was a woman of action, though. Words, promises, she didn't trust.

Dex was transfixed by this woman as she led him into her house—if anyone could call the imposing structure that. More like an architect's wet dream.

"Damn. A castle in Las Vegas," he commented, drawing a rich chuckle from her.

"A castle? Not quite." She deposited her purse on a fat club chair and dropped her keys into a crystal leaf-shaped dish on a side table. She hung on to the airtight plastic container that held her cupcake.

"There's a turret, Danica."

Another laugh. "Well, okay. Castle-*esque*." She fiddled with a bank of switches, and in moments the room was awash in soft gold tones. The textured mahogany coffee table glowed as deeply and richly as a full-bodied wine.

"Bamboo stalks," he said, recognizing the ripples in the high-glossed surface. "Where'd you get this?"

"A friend of a friend of a friend knows an artisan in Europe. It was a wedding gift that I didn't send off to Christie's for auction." She neatened the fan of magazines atop the piece. "Become a music idol, and this, too, could be yours."

Dex watched her scan the surroundings with a frown. Classic beauty and luxury—everything a woman who appreciated the finest things in life should want. Yet she looked troubled.

"It's haunted, you know."

"Haunted?"

"Not really." She shrugged. "It was never exactly my vision of a home. It was made for entertaining. Now it doesn't serve even that purpose, since I work too much to take on hosting any get-togethers." She ran a finger over the top of a framed picture of a woman in a trench coat stepping out of a car, holding a gigantic umbrella against the rain. The shot looked as though it was pulled straight from an old Hollywood movie.

"Is that—" he stepped closer "—Tem? Your mother?"

"Give the man a prize," Danica said with a teasing smile. "Yes, it's her. The car she's getting out of? My sisters and I were in it. I remember this exact moment." She traced her mother's image lovingly. "I thought, if I could be so perfect, so adored...but I can't. Too many flaws. Too much to juggle."

"Faith House was started before the Blues bought the Slayers franchise. Why put so much on your plate?"

"I don't see it that way," she said. "My parents insisted that my instincts and specific skill set made me a perfect fit for GM. It's a position of power, and I'm not sorry I took it. My parents wouldn't entrust this level of responsibility to just anyone, and they want the best. No one's more committed to protecting my family's interests than I am."

What he wasn't hearing was what *she* wanted.

Danica patted the food container. "I'll put this on a dish." She vanished through an arched entryway. When she returned minutes later, she said, "Faith House is something I can call my own. It's really taking off, with the college counseling and the crisis shelter. Good things ahead."

There was pride in her voice, but wistfulness in her eyes.

"It helps me remember Faith."

"Was she a friend?"

"She attempted to mug me."

Dex stilled, then crossed his arms. "I'm gonna need some help connecting the dots, Danica."

"She was a sixteen-year-old who was so desperate for a way out of a gang and prostitution that she tried to mug a stranger for enough money to outrun her pimp. She said she had a weapon, I called her bluff and it turned out that she was just an unarmed, scared girl.

"I saw to it that Faith got help. An incredible difference it made, too. But in a few months, she was in a car that wasn't as safe as it should've been. It blew up on the highway." Danica cast her gaze at the cupcake. "The news referred to her as just another unfortunate kid whose life jumped the rails. She was more than that, and I took a chance because I believed in her. I still do."

Was that the same way she believed in him?

Danica extended the plate to him. "Couldn't find a candle small enough not to topple the cupcake. I figured since it's your birthday I'd give you the whole thing. It's a great, great sacrifice for a sweets addict such as myself."

"Have some," he said, and she didn't hesitate before swiping her finger through the crooked calligraphy *D* and scooping the frosting into her mouth.

She sat on the sofa, putting the coffee table between them as she swirled her tongue around her finger. Dex couldn't pry his stare from the slow, slick movement of her tongue curling around the digit. "Dex."

"What?"

"Don't forget to make a wish."

He looked directly in her eyes and swept his tongue over the frosting.

Her eyelashes fluttered. "What'd you wish for?"

Dex set the dish on the table. "A cold beer."

"Beer. I can do that. Fresh out of Utopias, though." Her head tilted, and her deep chocolate gaze stroked him. "I thought you'd wish for a kiss."

"If I had, would you have given it to me?"

Danica didn't blink for several heartbeats. Then she suddenly sprang off the sofa and vaulted herself onto the coffee table. The extra elevation had her hovering a few inches over him. She snaked one arm over his shoulder while the other hand cradled his jaw.

So many secrets swirled in her eyes, and he wanted to unlock every one.

Danica's body swayed into his, and as if on command his groin tightened. Another intimate gyration. Then an almost tortured moan sawed through her full lips before she brought them down to his.

He met her with his tongue, licking into her, savoring the sounds of their mouths tasting and taking. With a small sigh, Danica closed her lips around his tongue, sucking him to the tip before she withdrew from the kiss.

Fluidly hopping down from the table, she strutted from the room. "A cold beer. Coming up."

Every centimeter of Dex's body vibrated with need so intense it was audible, surging in his ears. The house was quiet except for the cadence of Danica's shoes striking the floor. The sound lured him to an expansive kitchen that was set in shadows except for the lone light pouring from the open refrigerator.

Danica emerged, shutting the door with a bump of

her hip and smoothly moving toward the entryway. She stopped when she saw him filling the space. "Hey."

Accepting the drink, he turned the bottle up for a long swallow that quenched absolutely nothing. He set down the bottle and twisted back around.

When he banded an arm around her waist, she went willingly, pressing that taut body against his. One step backward. Then another. Then more. Like drumbeats, he felt them in his core as he walked her backward across the room.

Danica's back met the refrigerator, and he braced his arms on the cool surface, one on either side of her head. He went for her mouth, taking her warm tongue in deep as he peeled away her jacket. Roughly he ridded her of shoes, top, bra and pants, then grasped the crotch of her thong and stretched it so that the silky strip grazed her smooth folds. Finally, he slid it down her legs.

Danica's hand roamed down her body, and he almost came in his jeans at the sound of her finger exploring her wetness. Dex rolled his tongue over her nipples, learning their texture, before he took her hand and sucked her damp finger into his mouth. He let her taste coat his tongue, instantly addicted. "If you're going to turn back and grab on to those rules, now's the time to do it, Danica."

She shifted her hips forward to meet his, giving him an answer. He pulled a condom from his pocket and unzipped his jeans to free himself. Danica's hands gripped his shoulders as he grabbed her ass and boosted her high against the refrigerator. Magnets popped off the stainless steel, clattering onto the floor. Papers crumpled and floated down.

Dex speared her tight, wet heat. The answering moan she made against his lips almost unraveled what little restraint he had left.

She spoke, just two words, punctuated with the whimpers his thrusts pulled from her. "I'm…yours…"

Then, in a wave of hard spasms, she broke. Deep inside her, he fed off her pleasure, and in moments he followed her release with his own.

Eventually he was able to let her go, setting her gently on her feet. Dex got rid of the condom, then wandered to the counter where he'd left the beer. He damn near drained the bottle.

Not enough. Claiming her against a refrigerator wasn't enough. Not by a goddamn long shot.

He heard a rustle of fabric as Danica kicked her clothes across the floor and moved through the shadows. All of a sudden, light engulfed the room. Squinting to adjust his vision to the brightness, he whirled away from the counter.

Danica waited near the entryway. Naked. Mouth swollen. Hair a sexy mess. Honey-brown skin shimmering with sweat. "What now?"

"Now—" Dex wound his arms around her, sweeping her up slowly until they were eye to eye "—I take what's mine."

Chapter 11

As hot as refrigerator banging was, Danica knew it was only an introduction to what limits they could push. A warning of a potency that was rawer than screwing, deeper than lovemaking, more complicated than sex.

She wanted him to touch her until she was thirsty, starved and too spent to move. Now that she was in his arms, digging her heels into his ass, gauging his readiness for more by pumping her body tight onto his crotch, she thought she was off to a good start.

"This is the second time I've been naked in this kitchen today," she confessed.

He exhaled onto her throat. "God. Is that a habit?"

"Uh-uh. Could *make* it one."

"Move in with me."

Danica angled herself to kiss his temple. "No."

Dex carried her out of the kitchen as if she were a Fabergé egg—precious, tiny, delicate. She loved that he could hold her. It was a longed-for change; even she grew weary of standing on her own two feet *all the time*. But she wasn't a jeweled egg, and tonight she didn't want to be handled with caution. She wanted the full force of his passion. They might be mismatched in height, size and brawn, but she was looking forward to taking him on.

Abruptly, she threw her arms up.

She slid an inch or two down his body and he tightened his hold to keep from dropping her. "What the hell was that?"

"Put me down." Danica wriggled out of his embrace, grabbed the front of his shirt in her fists. "Come after me. Up the stairs. Let's go."

Dex was a step behind her the entire way to her bedroom. At the door, she grunted as he suddenly bent to squeeze her bum.

"I don't know which I like more," he muttered. "Your ass..." He spread her cheeks, shook them. "Or your breasts..." He dragged his hands up to pinch her nipples. "Or what about down here?"

He twisted first one, then two fingers into her. Danica shut her eyes, sighing in dirty delight. The authority he had with her body was unexpected, yet it shouldn't have been. Hadn't the way he'd taken her with his eyes on the balcony at Slayers Club Lounge put her on notice?

Danica clumsily opened her bedroom door—only to remember how messy she'd left it this morning, as though her closet had upchucked clothes all over the bed. She snatched the door shut. "New plan. We can't go in there."

"Why not?"

"It's not fit for guests."

"I'm not a guest. I'm a man who wants *you*. If we go in there, I swear I'll be looking only at you. And I'm not after a perfect woman. I'm after pushy, klutzy, sexy-as-hell Danica Blue."

Sexy as hell was flattering. *Pushy,* not so much—even if it was true. *Klutzy,* that was uncalled for. "I'm not klutzy." She preceded him into the bedroom, making a dash for the designer-label pileup on the four-poster bed.

"Argumentative. I should've added that one," he said, and when she pivoted to give him a profane gesture, he whipped off his shirt. At his collar was a cross on a silver chain.

Danica was struck dumb by the definition of muscle and bone and the symmetry of his body. She wished she could zap her mattress clear and push him onto it.

She turned to scoop up a handful of garments, but misjudged the distance. Clotheslined at the thighs, she landed bent over on the bed with a stunned *"Oooppphhh!"*

Great way to prove *his* point.

Dex was on her, flipping her onto her back, taking full advantage of her position. The abrasion of the scruff on his jaw was a marriage of pleasure and pain on her sensitive flesh. Spreading her legs wider, he lapped her moist slit.

A very *im*proper oath slipped past her mouth and she dropped her hands onto her face.

"No, Danica. No holding back. First, to take care of this..." Dex helped her off the bed. He yanked the four corners of her comforter toward the middle of the bed, trapping all the clothes inside, and slung the bundle onto the floor. "Now say what you want."

Danica boldly stared him down. "You—naked and inside me."

Dex stripped swiftly, and the sight of his rigid cock had her lowering to her knees. She went for his balls, tested the weight of them in her mouth, before she feasted languidly on his erection.

"Your mouth," he growled, withdrawing from her. "Definitely your mouth is what I like best." Then he went completely still. "Crap. I don't have another condom."

Danica almost fainted in relief. "I'm all over it." She crawled across the mattress to her nightstand and fished for the party favors from Veda's bachelorette party. She dumped the contents onto the bed and counted the foil packets. Six. Well, that *might* get them through the night. "I want to use everything in this bag. Think you can help me do that?"

He responded with a kiss that sucked the sense out of her. Bringing his sinewy body down on hers, he watched her face. His smoldering gaze trapped hers. Driving slowly and deeply into her, he held her.

Three foil packets, a silk blindfold and a shower that had been more dirty than cleansing later, panic caught her. Danica had pulled on the first article of clothing she saw—a ruffled red shirt that was long enough to cover her hips—and was untying the blindfold from one of the bed's posts when it dawned that she was in it deep.

With each climax, each stroke of his talented hands on her body, she only ached for him more intensely. It wasn't supposed to work that way. They were on borrowed time together; neither had the right to expect the passion they found—or created—in each other to bleed into the real world. Danica's carefully structured life had no room in it for a spontaneous man who coaxed her down from the pedestal she'd been perched on for so long. She had no plan in place to guard herself against the consequences of yearning for more than one night.

What a fantastically dumb-ass mistake it was to let lust lead them this far. Because now, as Danica lowered to all fours in search of her Valentino pumps—where were they, anyway?—she was finally afraid of something. Afraid that lust might abandon her on love's doorstep.

Dex had come into her life without a warning, and damn it, it wasn't fair. They were supposed to be on opposite sides. But what had that led to?

Plenty of sex, and emotions she hadn't a clue what to do with. The possibility that she couldn't think her way out of a predicament ramped up her fear.

Head to the floor, rump in the air, Danica peered beneath her bed. No shoes. Ugh.

So, *this* was what happened when you free-fell and hit the bottom....

"Not that watching your ass isn't getting me hot," Dex's voice said from behind her, "but is there a reason you're down there?"

Danica turned over onto her back on the floor. "My shoes are missing." She gazed up at him—he was wickedly gorgeous standing there in just his jeans—as tears swamped her eyes.

Joining her on the floor, he said, "There's a pair in your kitchen, along with the rest of what you had on."

Oh. "Right. I forgot. I'm forgetting everything that matters."

"You're regretting what we're doing."

"What *are* we doing, Dex? *I* don't do things like this. Careless risks, rule-breaking, they aren't in my repertoire." When she swiped her palms over her eyes, they came away smudged with tears. "What's next? We make a clean break? I go on playing one part for the public, and another for you?"

"Compartmentalizing doesn't work in every situation."

"Not true. 'A place for everything, and everything in its place.'"

"Then what's my place?"

Somewhere in her life. Where, exactly, she had no idea. Naturally, he didn't make things easy for her, so he didn't fit neatly into the "friend" or "lover" compartments. But maybe if she amended them to "unlikely friend" and "inappropriate lover"?

"I haven't worked out the kinks yet," she said.

"You don't have a designated spot in my life, Danica."

Danica held herself in check, refusing to let the words bruise her. "No?"

"You exist there, and the possibilities of what you could mean to me are open. Anything can happen. Or not. Either way, I don't expect something you can't give."

"Roll with it," she deduced. "Sounds like a defense mechanism."

"Better than pinning your hopes on something and watching them be shot down. As for us…" He picked up her hand and gently kissed her knuckles while stroking her with a roguish look, making her feel simultaneously like a pure maiden and a decadent harlot "…the only way you can control exactly how far we get into this is if you tell me right now that it stops here. Want it to stop?"

Here was her out, an opportunity to chalk up crossing the line with Dex as a one-night mistake. A proper girl's lapse in erotic judgment. *Yes,* she thought, *I want it to stop.* "No," she said instead. "I don't want it to stop."

She gave a shaky smile as he thumbed away her tears.

"Cry when you need to, Danica," he said after a moment. "Get pissed off. Get excited. All of that you can do with me. Trust me on that."

She already did. Before she'd even been ready to, she'd trusted him. She kissed him softly. "Thank you for catching me when I was falling."

Confusion passed through his blue eyes, then he grinned.

"Oh. When you were about to do a face-plant with that cake at the Mandarin."

Okay, that, too. "Yeah." She reached to finger the cross dangling from his neck. "Is there a story behind this?"

"It was my grandfather's."

"When did he give it to you?"

"He didn't. My dad did, when I was gearing up to leave Oregon. We weren't speaking, but he handed me this the last time I saw him. Sometimes I like to think that things were okay with us that last day…but I'd already let him down and hadn't really found a way to make it right."

Danica wanted to get up and point out that he was wearing tangible proof that he'd had parents who'd loved him in spite of their disagreements. And he had a sister who'd probably long ago forgiven and forgotten.

He had more to offer than even he was willing to see.

It was simply up to her to show him. Somehow.

Game-day predictions had the Slayers securing a fifth consecutive win, closing the weekend undefeated at 5–0. To be the subject of the NFL's hottest scandal *and* on a victory spree was enough to—as Martha had put it when Danica had joined her in the press box for a halftime interview and a round of sangrias—put an ass in every seat.

Fans of the red-and-silver, who had faith in the Blues' take-no-prisoners approach to business, accredited the wins to new blood in the front office and on the field. Skeptics said the team had been riding high on luck and hype, and both would fold once the Slayers confronted a mature, consistent championship-winning ball club.

Hosting the AFC East's current dominant team, and disadvantaged with a defense that wasn't yet in total sync because of a newly acquired defensive tackle and cornerback, replacements for the men in those positions who'd played during Al Franco's reign as owner, Las Vegas had the chips stacked against it.

Midway through the fourth quarter, Danica retreated from the windows of the owners' box and faced her mother, who stood motionless in a stance emanating power and elegance. Tem's business suit was black and simple— would've been dreary if not for the stylish Slayers-red ribbons on the cuffs and collar. It was an appropriately somber ensemble considering the team's winning streak was on the verge of ending, thanks to an offense that had choked in the pocket and a receiver who'd fumbled and failed to recover…three times. Each turnover had resulted in the opponent scoring, and at a twenty-one-point deficit with under seven left in the final quarter, the matchup was, for all intents and purposes, over.

"I'm going onto the field to stand with Pop," Danica told Tem.

Tem's executive assistant, the administration coordinator and the half dozen chattering guests who'd been welcomed into the suite on the owners' personal invitation were transparently more concerned with eating, drinking and being merry than the actual football game. She went to a mirror to touch up her makeup. "Ma, I'll stick around when Kip goes to the podium post-game, so I won't be back in the suite until afterward."

Tem's answer was a tense bow of her head as she looked out over the field.

"Ma, four-to-one isn't an execution. Play-offs are still a possibility."

"Good enough—that's what I'm hearing from you." Tem revolved leisurely on her sedate designer heels, but her eyes were alight with angry sparks. The others in the room chose this moment to snap to attention. "Five-to-zero is perfection. Victory in the play-offs is perfection.

All of the money Marshall and I are spending, all of the strategizing, it has a purpose that we expect our general manager to agree wholeheartedly with. We won't be placated with *good enough* when a championship is at stake."

Danica didn't realize she'd been frozen by the assault until her mother announced she was going to the telephone that was a direct line to the field. "What are you instructing?"

"That the slippery-fingered running back get comfortable on the bench. I'm going to want someone else in—permanently. Of course, you'll take care of this? Make it clean, but be sure the message is clear to all of our offense. As for now, we have a time-out remaining, and it's our possession."

Danica knew what she was hoping for: a touchdown, an interception with a touchdown and yet another touchdown. It wasn't exactly impossible, but the odds of Danica strutting across the field wearing nothing but flip-flops were higher.

"Corday isn't going to drive the ball, Ma. He isn't a confident reader on the field, and that's no secret. If he takes the risks you're crossing your fingers for, he'll botch a play."

"Playing it safe got us a three-touchdown deficit! To be slaughtered in our house is unacceptable." Tem placed two fingertips between her eyes, massaging away a frown crease. She addressed the administration coordinator, Antoine Isaiah. "Go."

Antoine veered into the debate. "In these circumstances, twenty-one in the hole, it's a matter of pride versus desperation. If we have too much pride to attempt a drive, get our men downfield and get Corday to throw long, then we're guaranteed this loss. If we're desperate enough—which I say we are with four and change on the game clock—

then we risk losing pride, but we might get the yardage and points we want."

"You're both oversimplifying this," Danica argued. "Ma, listen to me. Pop and Kip have made every necessary adjustment in this game. What you're not seeing are sloppy receivers and a quarterback whose accuracy is already handicapped by an injury. When Brock Corday is confident in his passes, he does not make a mistake. If you force Brock to start throwing wildly, it'll affect his mental and physical preparedness. I know him. I brought him on board."

"Yes, you brought us a captain who won't take chances," Tem said.

"Brock takes a chance every time he suits up. Pop and Kip are on the field. They're capable. They can see what those of us all cozy in this suite can't see. I'm going to join them. After the game I'll visit the locker room."

"A little guidance, Danica. Skip the camaraderie. Be direct."

"Bust balls, you mean." A cool lift of a meticulously arched eyebrow answered her. "Gauging a situation and determining the best approach is my specialty, Ma. I don't need to be handled like a ventriloquist dummy."

Tem braced her hands on her hips. "Marshall and I have a partnership. We own and control this franchise jointly."

"We're all a *team,* Ma." Something inside Danica crumbled at the fact that she had to remind her mother of that. What was Danica's authority if she was vetoed at every turn? "Don't make that call. Let your GM and coach do this."

Danica went to the door, but when she turned back, her mother was already moving in her pageant-perfected gait toward the adjoining soundproofed room with the phone.

The elevator was vacant when Danica stepped inside.

Here she was, once again confronted with the pull-the-rug-out-from-under-you sort of change she hated. There was no one to vent to. Nothing to punch. So she screamed.

Her screech echoed off every surface of the elevator and had her ears ringing by the time the elevator doors ushered her to the ground floor. On the way out to the field, she swiped a Slayers on-field ball cap, put it on and tugged her ponytail through the opening in the back. Then she marched outside to join the Slayers staff, players and her family on the sidelines.

Marshall was pacing, studying the play in progress, so Danica slipped past him to mingle with the benched players. The hulking men dwarfed her, but she was never intimidated by their size, put off by their less-than-refined manners, or offended by dirt and gritty language.

This was a business that her family was running, and while she was counted on to be fresh and photo-ready, she didn't think a finicky attitude had a place in this game. It was a brutal sport that tortured the toughest of men.

Picking her way over the turf to the special teams coach, Danica asked, "How is TreShawn?" as her gaze located the kicker warming up his lean frame. TreShawn Dibbs was in his early twenties but had let god-awful decisions age him. He was a man her sister Charlotte had taken under her wing during training camp in Mount Charleston. It was a connection that warranted gossip and that Danica and her parents still weren't completely convinced was the most beneficial for the lone female athletic trainer, but Charlotte had dug her heels in and formed a friendship of sorts with TreShawn.

And as long as his performance exceeded projections and expectations, Danica wouldn't interfere with a winning formula.

"Solid," the coach told her, squinting against the Nevada sunshine. "Stable."

"All good, then." Danica poured herself a cup of Gatorade and migrated to the trainers.

"Hey, sis." Charlotte, in her crisp trainer uniform, with her curly mane of hair wrangled into a messy braid and a serious woman-on-the-job expression on her face, snapped a wad of bubble gum. Her eyes fixed on the field, she said, "I think a call just came from the owners' suite."

"The queen's ruling the land from her tower." The comment earned her a glance rife with questions. "I didn't mean that."

"Danica…just when you show signs of life, show a smidgen of moxie, you backpedal. Remember when the three of us girls were little, and we'd play double Dutch? Martha and I were the only ones who'd actually play. Every single time you got ready to jump, you'd hesitate and give up. You never will jump in, will you?"

Grateful that the late-afternoon breeze cooled her hot-with-embarrassment skin, Danica swallowed down the comeback that she'd *jumped* plenty all last night with the team's former quarterback. "I'd rather maintain a positive relationship with our folks, instead of doing things that drive Pop to antacids and Ma to frown. She hates frowning, you know."

Charlotte turned to her. "Um…yes, I know. But she's the one who insisted on getting each of us rodent after rodent and goldfish after goldfish as pets when we were kids so we'd be desensitized to death." She shrugged. "Ma and Pop should both know how to cope with loss. But she's up in the suite throwing a hissy fit, and Pop looks like he wants to put on a helmet and play his damn self."

"I'll make sure he won't," Danica assured her. "After the game, why don't you, Martha and I have dinner with them? It's been months since we've all sat down around a table without tears or bloodshed."

Bloodshed referring to Charlotte shoving away from the table in offense to their parents' criticism, and Martha dropping a glass and suffering a deep laceration when she'd tried to pick up the shards. The result was that their parents continued to bring up the incident when it served their purpose of guilt-tripping Charlotte, Martha had developed a fear of handling broken glass and Danica had been unaffected.

"Martha and I can't," Charlotte said, her gaze continuing to track the players. "Nate's treating us to a show at Caesars."

"I haven't been to Caesars Palace in a while." Wistfulness gushed from her words, but she hoped the thousands of voices up in the bleachers could mask it.

"Oh. Danica, we didn't mean to exclude you...." Charlotte sighed. "But that's what we did, and I apologize for the ass-hattery."

"Charlotte, never apologize when you're not sorry. You taught me that. FYI, I never jumped because you swung your end of the ropes too fast, and Martha swung hers too low."

A childish barb, but it was salve for her hurt feelings as she turned and walked to Marshall and the band of coaches stalking about. For the remainder of the game she stayed in the safety of her father's shadow; then she was swallowed up into the chaos as, like waters breaking through a dam, players and personnel and the press converged onto the field for handshakes, post-game interviews and photos.

After Kip's press conference and a tense visit to the locker room, she escaped to the owners' suite with her mind set on apologizing for being short with her mother earlier. Danica arrived to find everyone still there except

Tem. Instead, Martha was perched on the tufted settee that Tem usually occupied. "Ma around, Martha?"

"Little girls' room." Martha scooped a toasted brioche with caviar from a tray of appetizers. "If you're going that way, would you please deliver her cell? It's vibrating itself into a seizure. Plus, she's probably going crazy wondering where she left it."

Danica grabbed the phone as it vibrated again. The name and number displayed on the caller ID stopped her short. A cold sweat surfaced on her skin as the phone rattled in her grip.

"Don't answer it." Martha crossed the room quickly. "Ma would fry anyone—including the favorite daughter—for answering her phone."

"I'm answering it."

Martha's eyes bugged. "Fun time's over, y'all." The guests and staff voiced reluctance but cleared the room quickly on her orders.

Watching her sister shut the door—with her on the wrong side of it, wiggling her eyebrows expectantly—Danica slid her thumb across the phone's screen. "Marion."

"Marion?" Martha echoed, butting her head against Danica's in her haste to scoot in close enough to hear. "Why is *he* calling?"

"Who's this?" Marion demanded.

"After ten years of marriage and a year of you in my grill at every turn, I'd think you would recognize my voice. All I really care about is why you're calling my mother."

"Ask Tem and Marshall. Ask them why I'm calling. Ask your parents why I'm there, in your face, 'at every turn,' Danni."

Danica turned away from Martha, putting out a hand to maintain distance. "Right now it's you who's in the hot seat. No lies. Just the truth. You owe me that much, damn it."

"Lay out the truth, huh? Let me ask you this. Did Tem ask you about the writing you had on your arm that night at the Marquee?"

"No." But on the night Danica joined Tem and Willa for dinner at the Bellagio, Tem *had* studied her closely, as though searching for something specific. "Did you tell my mother that I'd gotten a tattoo?"

"I told her and Marshall that I suspected you've been hooking up with someone, and he wrote on your arm." Marion sighed into the phone, the sound ragged and stripped. "It was juvenile. I was operating on straight emotion. I wanted to be done with this shit."

Danica's gaze followed her sister as she opened the suite's door to Tem.

"You've got the answers, Danni. Accept them. I knew you were going to be at the club with your assistant not because I'm clairvoyant. Your. Parents. Told. Me. Ever since the divorce, I've been in your face because *they* told me to be."

Tem snatched the phone and killed the call. "What right do you have to invade my privacy this way, Danica? I think less of you now."

"Even less than you did when you thought I was sleeping with a guy who wasn't approved by you and Pop?"

"How dare you?"

"Speak the truth? We should all try that more often, instead of tiptoeing around it. So I'll start. I am aware that the only reason you and Pop didn't interfere with my relationship with Ollie was that his aunt is a member of your country club."

"Ollie was interested in a real relationship, but you were too stupidly spoiled to give him a chance."

Danica was stunned to her core. But as she'd told Dex, words—even ones spoken by her mother, with the intent to maim her pride—were only words. She could survive them.

"I didn't want a relationship fresh off of a divorce. You and Pop acted as if you understood that."

"We figured you'd dumped Ollie because you hadn't moved on from Marion. We watched you suffer the consequences of what that man had done to you. You didn't even have an escort to Veda's wedding."

"My God. *That's* how you knew. Marion sang like a bird to you, didn't he?"

Tem straightened her spine. "We were protecting you and making him see that he has an obligation to you that we expect him to honor. This is how you thank us? By being argumentative?"

"What should she say?" Martha interjected. "'Thanks for trying to put me back into an unfaithful marriage'?"

"Not another word from you, Martha Blue." Tem's stare bored into her youngest daughter. "Be relieved that you're not the topic of conversation. Neither you nor I can accurately name the number of men that the tabloids have linked you to this year. Your *popularity* with men doesn't bode well for your future in a male-dominated sport, don't you agree?"

Martha snickered. What type of resilience must she have to just let the dagger-sharp criticism ping off her? "I never kiss and tell."

"Not necessary, my darling. The masses of men who look at you with pure sex in their eyes are telling enough. Putting you into a respectable career, giving you a home with family, is proof that we haven't turned our backs on you. Count your blessings, Martha, because between Charlotte taking up with Nate Franco and Danica carrying on with God knows who, I don't have the energy or inclination to reel you back into line. But just keep in mind that your day of reckoning with your father and me is coming. Soon." Tem held out her phone, waving it. "This man did you a disservice, Danica. Marshall and I made it clear to him that when he married you, he entered into a contract with binding conditions. And even though the legal system let him slip free, we're not so forgiving. We encouraged him to take you back."

"Take *me* back?"

"Cheating on you is the same as discarding you. So yes, take you back."

"Well, fuck me for putting a wrinkle in your plans."

Martha and Tem gasped in unison. Their ears weren't delicate; they simply had never heard Danica use such harsh profanity.

Marshall entered the suite, immediately reading the tension that crisscrossed the room. "Did he stir up something?" he directed to his wife.

"Call him by his name, Pop," Danica said. "Marion called Ma's phone, I answered and got him to talk. All along it's been you and Ma stirring things up. You have zero say in my relationship with him. We're divorced, and that's not going to change."

"Being divorced has done you no favors." Tem went to stand at Marshall's side. "Even Veda downgraded you from matron of honor to bridesmaid, and the good Lord couldn't have blessed you with a more loyal and caring friend. All this change, Danica, is changing you, and I don't like it."

"Charlotte and Martha are the secret-keepers, not you," Marshall added, and Martha's eyes narrowed in offense. "You were married, settled. We knew what to expect from you. Whatever he found carousing with other women can't replace the friendship you and he had. Be mature, Danica. Don't turn down a chance to make things right with your husband just for the sake of overblown self-respect."

"*Ex*-husband," she corrected vehemently, storming past the three of them. "This conversation ends here. I'll be with Kip in the auditorium, asking the offensive men we acquired why they can't protect the damn ball. After that, my office door is open to any of you. But please, approach me with team business only."

Tem blocked the doorway, clasping Danica's face gently in her hands. "It's been a difficult day for us all, Danni. I'm willing to forgive the way you spoke to me."

"Don't give me something I don't want." The words, infused with honesty, were almost painful to say. "I am changing. I can feel it as surely as you see it happening."

And I'm glad.

Chapter 12

"Epic mistake, or brilliant move. Which one are you?" Danica asked the email she'd just drafted.

The email on Danica's iPad, of course, offered no commentary. Once released into the jungles of cyberspace, the message waiting in limbo in her drafts folder would hopefully trigger two results: reconcile Dex with his sister and get the league's attention—in a *positive* way.

"Kill two birds with one stone" was the idiom her father was fond of. But since Danica still occasionally mourned the first pet finch Marshall and Tem had given her to love and lose, she didn't prefer the phrase.

Whether her scheme proved worthwhile or backfired depended on Dex's sister. Last night, it had been child's play to find Erin Harper online. Everything from her college-graduation announcement in *The Gunner Chronicle* to her YouTube channel was available for public access. In the time it had taken Danica to eat chicken chow mein in her kitchen office, she'd found a home-organization blog, an email address and an active phone number registered to Erin.

Just now, in her stadium office, she'd composed a message from one of her personal email addresses. She'd already gotten through to the right contacts at ESPN, so all she needed to do was scrape up the nerve to hit Send.

Her plan was to get Dex and his sister on an ESPN Films *30 for 30* documentary. Working on the project would retie familial bonds. It would be a story of a young man's reconciliation with his family, of a quarterback's redemption. It would be sellable, and the ace he needed to get back on top.

It would be proof that yes, she was that damn good.

And what she and Dex had would end once she helped him get what he wanted. It didn't seem fair that while she had him in her life, they had to keep it a secret. Selfishly, she wanted to flaunt to the world that—at least for now— he belonged to her.

In times of question, her best friend put faith in waiting for a sign to point her toward the right path. On the day that Veda had at last accepted Mekhi Corrine's marriage proposal, she'd received a "You've been preapproved!" offer from MasterCard in the mail and was confident that seeing his initials was indubitably a sign that she should take the plunge.

Danica set the tablet on her desk to rummage the tray of spiritual stones Veda had gifted her after Danica's divorce. Valor. Confidence. Protection. Passion.

She put the tray down. She was all right in the *passion* department—if this morning's two-orgasm quickie with Dex was any indication.

A tap on the door snapped her out of a sensual replay of the moves he'd used to leave her feeling sinful, sated and ready to do a touchdown dance. Danica sat reed-straight in her plush chair and motioned Lilith into the office.

"Got the physician's reports for Shankman and Knowles," Lilith said, approaching the desk.

The owners had called for stat physicals for the second- and third-string quarterbacks following this past Sunday's loss. Now that the team had reached its bye week, Marshall and Tem were taking the time to regroup and strategize while many rested up.

"Would you forward it, please?"

"Did. Twenty minutes ago."

Danica scrunched her face in a frown, realizing belatedly that she hadn't stopped to smooth the creases away. To prep herself for the last-minute staff meeting at five on the dot, she'd need to review the reports.

She scanned her desk, making sure that she hadn't printed them already. Neatly organized appointment book. Color-coded directory. Two coordinated calendars.

"It didn't come through, Lilith."

"Odd. Could it have gone to spam?" Without pausing for an answer, Lilith plucked the tablet from the desk and started tapping the screen. "Get this one on its way. Now let's check your in-box—"

"Lil, that's not my work tablet—"

"Oh, screw." Lilith lowered the device. "I'm so sorry."

Danica reached for the tablet and checked her sent messages. The most recent was from her account to Erin Harper's. "I…uh…wasn't ready to pull the trigger on that email yet."

Lilith looked mortified. "I'm going to forward the other one again. Boss, I really am sorry."

"No worries, Lil." Danica's heart was racing, but whether with dread or anticipation, she wasn't certain. She spied the tray of stones. Well. How was *that* for a sign?

After the meeting, Danica holed up in her office and worked. Nervous jitters did wonders for her productivity, but once every item on her team business to-do list was complete, she—in completely twisted curiosity—opened *Minesweeper* on her computer.

The fourth game-over explosion had her calling the PR department and summoning her sister to the managers' wing. A bit of Martha therapy would distract her from dwelling neurotically on the outcomes of contacting Dex's sister. She hadn't invaded his privacy; she'd reached out to his family as part of an effort to hold up her end of their bargain. She was just being a good friend.

Chances of him seeing it that way? Slim. But it was a gamble she'd pursued for his sake.

Martha entered the office without knocking. "You rang?"

"God. The Lurch impersonation needs practice."

"Just getting into the Halloween spirit. All that's creepy, spooky, indecent and depraved is up my alley."

"Yeah…I'd be choosy about who I advertise that to."

Her sister smirked. "So, what's the problem? Why am I here?" Danica's expression must've reflected offense, because Martha added, "Seriously, you only invite me to your office when there's a problem. At first I thought it'd be kind of fun to work in the same building—that we'd hang out in each other's offices. Sort of like being kids again and visiting each other's rooms. Oh, except you never let me visit yours. So that leads me to ask you, *again,* why am I here?"

Well, that came full circle, didn't it? "I just wanted to chat. But if you're busy—"

"Not." Martha had no reservations about making herself comfortable. Gathering provisions from the mini fridge—chips, salsa and the fluffy pastry Danica had intended to take home with her—Martha made a nesting spot for herself on a corner of the desk. "Ma and Pop still miffed at you about the Marion stuff?"

If Danica were in the mood to be technical, she'd point out that it was *she* who possessed the right to be miffed at *them*. But the details didn't matter so much anymore. "Apologies were exchanged and we're focusing on the team."

"Then all is well in the king, queen and princess's court?"

Princess? As in excluding Charlotte and Martha? The words had come out naturally, without even a hint of snark. Only matter-of-factness. Danica was Marshall and Tem's favorite daughter; that was always painfully clear even to her. But that, too, was changing. She cleared her throat, yet it still felt constricted. "Everything's fine."

"The renovations are almost done on the new place. Ma and Pop insist on staying at the Bellagio until everything is moved in."

"You don't sound excited for a twenty-two-year-old who is days away from having an entire wing of a Vegas lakefront mansion."

"Eh." Scoop. Crunch. Crunch. Swallow. "It's an upgrade. Sort of like going from maximum security to minimum security. Still prison."

Danica couldn't disguise her sigh. Would Martha have the same sentiments if she really knew the gap between wealth and poverty in her own city? "Ungrateful and unfair, Martha. Bad combo."

"But that's how I feel about it. Our parents, Charlotte and now you—you guys all act as if I need to be monitored. You want to know where I go, who I'm with, what I do, what I'm feeling. Y'all act as if what I feel even matters. But it doesn't. People who say I'm important to them don't ever consult me *before* they do something. They just do it, and ask later, as an effin' afterthought, how it makes me feel."

"I can't speak for them. As your older sister, I have a duty—"

Martha snorted. "Didn't your sisterly duty expire on your wedding day?"

"Oh, so there *is* some resentment there. I thought you were just naturally a pain in my ass." Danica reached to swipe the pastry from her sister's junk-food stockpile. "And give me my cream puff. I ate rice cakes and cherries for lunch, holding out for this."

"Danica, I'm going to say this calmly, okay? You said 'I do' to being Marion's wife and 'I don't' to being my sister. When Charlotte was in college, doing her own thing, it was you and me. Then Marion got into the picture, and you married him without ever asking how it might make me feel to lose you."

"Martha, that's a distorted way to see it."

"Lovely. The lawyer-y talk." She brushed a crumb from her painted-on checkered pants. "I'm not a kid anymore, though, and the scab fell off that wound eons ago. The point is, I was left to manage my feelings alone then and I can do so now."

So much for Martha therapy.

Despite the flaring tempers, Martha remained on the desk, putting a decent dent in the bag of chips. When Lilith knocked, she scarcely glanced up.

"Got a visitor outside," Lilith announced, then she dropped her voice. "I know he's got a rep for being on the…intense…side, but I'm getting the 'royally pissed off' vibe from him."

"Who is it?" Danica asked, rising from her chair.

"Dex Harper," Lilith replied.

Martha's head snapped up, and Danica watched Lilith welcome him into the office. He muttered, "Thank you" to Lilith, who beamed as she left. He gave a hitch of his chin to Martha, who inadvertently nipped her fingertip while crunching on a chip as her round gaze tracked him.

"Danni," her sister said, untwisting herself from her perch on the desk, not once losing sight of their visitor, "so that thing you told me to be choosy about who I advertised it to... Can I choose *him?*"

"No."

Martha glared at her, deflated. "Then can I have the cream puff?"

Danica slid the pastry over, which Martha promptly carried off with her.

Closing the door behind her sister, Danica gathered up the chip bag and salsa jar. "Let's get to it," she said to Dex. "You're riled up, and you have a bone to pick with me. Prolonging it isn't going to get us to a resolution any sooner."

"Are you for real?" His pitch was so low, so rough, that Danica paused at the mini fridge. "You piss on my explicit instructions to leave my sister alone, and you talk like it's business as usual. Gunner, my family, they're *my* business—not yours."

Danica had hoped that Erin Harper would reply to her before contacting her brother, but she couldn't blame the woman for being suspicious or alarmed that the GM who'd fired him was interested in resurrecting his career. "I only asked Erin if she'd be interested in meeting with me. She's a grown woman—you do realize that, right? She's a home-organization guru. I subscribed to her YouTube channel."

"Danica."

"The point is, Erin's capable of making her own decisions. So...what did she decide? Obviously she discussed this with you."

"She booked a flight to Vegas."

"That's great."

Dex stepped in front of her to stop her from buzzing about the office. Being on the move was the only way to resist looking at the soul-deep fury and disappointment in his eyes. She'd braced herself for whatever irate words he might sling her way, but she hadn't anticipated that he would look at her in such a hurt way.

"The safest place for Erin is in Oregon, away from the mess I made of my own life," he said. "Thanks to you, she now thinks she has the leverage to make demands. She wants to stick around this city, spend time with me."

"Which you won't agree to. No shocker there."

Dex took a half step, forcing her to move back until her booty encountered the desk. And then she was hemmed in with him leaning toward her, his hands planted on either side of her. "I get to be livid here. You and I and your family may be cool with the Las Vegas and NFL spotlight, but my parents? They didn't sign up for this. They never would've wanted Erin to follow in my footsteps."

"That's up to her to decide, though. She seems to think it's a good idea."

"It's carelessness that she can't afford. She's on pure desperation, trying to get to me."

Danica raised her chin. "Ask yourself why. Then, when you're ready to apologize to me for storming into my space all worked up when I'm only trying to help, ask me why I even reached out to her."

"That's a question you won't get, because there won't be an apology."

"*Riiiight.* The Blue-Eyed Badass doesn't apologize, how could I forget?" Danica pushed his shoulder, and when the solid muscle didn't budge and his hot stare didn't even waver from hers, she shoved hard with the heels of both hands. No effect, as though she were striking a brick wall with a feather.

Danica's hands fluttered, searching for some softness, some weakness on his body. The quest only discovered more hard planes, chiseled angles. Her fingers settled behind his neck, interlocked through his dark hair and cradled his head, dragging him into her. Finally, his stare released her.

Because his mouth was on hers.

A kiss didn't do this—turn a woman inside out, shake her entire being, inject her with a cocktail of euphoria and fear. But his did.

The friction of his tongue stroking hers was enough to make her curl her fingers greedily into his hair. But then he used his teeth, sinking them into her bottom lip with the exact amount of pressure to lure a reveal-all moan from her.

Where the strength to end the contact came from, Danica wasn't sure. Slapping her hands against his shoulders, she tore away from his mouth, and he slinked across the room. She watched him as he cast an annoyed look downward at his erection and cursed.

He was frustrated with himself for wanting her. Yeah, she could relate.

Teeth gritted, heart skittering, Danica growled, "I am not doing this to hurt you. I care, you damn jerk." She grabbed the folder with the ESPN Films information, thrust it toward him. "This was what I was working on— not that it makes a difference to you."

Dex took the folder and, without another word or glance, strode away.

Danica dropped back onto the edge of her desk, scrubbing at her lips as if to wipe the memory of his mouth from her tingling flesh.

"Boss?"

It was a challenge to discreetly lower her hand, straighten up and face her assistant. Lilith's gaze passed over her, and Danica saw the same note of realization that had sparked in the other woman's eyes when Marion asked if she'd recognized the signature on Danica's arm.

She knows.

But all Lilith said was, "If he comes here again...?"

Danica sat at her desk, closing the *Minesweeper* game on her computer. "He won't."

Damn it, Danica. Why couldn't you let it go?

Protecting his sister from the consequences of his choices by limiting their contact was what he'd done right—of that Dex was certain. Giving up that fight now that Erin, barely out of college and coddled all her life, was traipsing into his world—a world where people partied hard and screwed over their fellow man to hurdle to the top—was not an option.

Dex dragged his hands through his hair and walked over to his living-room windows, which offered a nighttime view of trees. This was as close to *remote* as a man could get in Las Vegas. Yeah, he'd craved the big city and had wanted to swim with the sharks, but once he'd gotten his wish and the time had come to claim territory, he'd picked an airy property away from the action. A location that offered the illusion of solitude, rural simplicity, something familiar that he was missing.

Restless, he reached into his pocket, jiggling the keys to his Corvette. He could meet his sister at the airport, turn her right back around on a flight home, and then what? He could find superficial company at any hot spot on the Strip. But with people like that he'd learned to keep his guard up. If nothing else, being ripped out of his career had helped him filter the double-crossers from the legit friends.

But Danica had passed that filter as well as the rest of his resistances.

A call to his friend and former teammate Russo Lewis and he'd be on the road to San Francisco. Russo's plans to be a bachelor for life had been shot to hell by a smokin' surgeon, but he'd sworn on his life that Dex would appreciate some time with California women.

But when his mind pictured the kind of woman who could get him worked up, she was delicate-framed, marched when she moved, paraded around town packing sex dice and massage oil…and she cared. About *him*.

Dex slowly turned to the folder she'd shoved at him. ESPN Films. A documentary, centered on him.

Did she genuinely care, or would he only be falling further into a game?

Before he could decide one way or another, Samantha showed up on his doorstep, absorbing all the space in his house with her man-trapping outfit, heady cover-up-the-cigarette-smoke perfume and loudmouthed laughter.

"Whoa, I hope the wrath sizzling off you isn't directed at me." She strolled into his house, swaying her denim-clad ass all the way to his kitchen, where she grabbed a jar of peanut butter from a cupboard, unscrewed the cap and poked her finger in.

"Double dip in that jar and it will be," he said. "That stuff's disgusting. What if I have people over, and they want peanut-butter-and-jelly sandwiches? Think they'll be all right with a touch of Samantha Weatherby's spit?"

Samantha pulled her peanut-butter-smeared finger from her mouth, making a soft popping sound. "You never had a problem with my spit when you kissed me."

"I knew what I was getting when I kissed you."

"If it's *that* much of an issue, I'll replace the whole jar." A few searches through drawers and cupboards rewarded her with a spoon, which she loaded with peanut butter. "Mmm. And no one I know over the age of thirteen offers peanut-butter-and-jelly sandwiches to guests."

"It was a what-if."

"A ridiculous one."

"Samantha, what's up with the drop-in? There's usually only one reason you randomly show up at my place."

She tossed her pink-streaked hair, glazing him with a brazen look. "Can't a girl veg out with a friend without having some ulterior motive?"

Not when that friend is me and you're clearly wearing a bra that does phenomenal things for your breasts.

It was her get-him-in-the-sack bra. It had never failed.

But there was a first time for everything....

"I think you're stressed," she diagnosed, her mouth pursed softly. "Can we park it on the porch? I was in a studio all day. Stir-crazy." She added a precocious smile. "Any of those Sam Adams Utopias left?"

"So you bought me a gift that you want for yourself."

"Is it my fault we have the same good taste in beer?" She unwound a gauzy scarf from her neck, already getting herself comfortable. "C'mon. I'm going out."

Dex let her claim a seat on the porch, then passed her a beer. He remained standing, arms crossed. "Be honest. Did it pan out with the man you hooked up with at that wedding?"

"No. I think, though, that you and I were hasty in calling it quits to our system."

"I'm not backsliding, Samantha. I don't want that kind of system anymore."

Samantha paused, peanut butter in one hand, beer in the other. "Unbelievable. It's happened...." She got up and pointed her bottle at the center of his chest. "Somebody's unlocked that."

"Saying my heart was locked up?"

"Mmm-hmm. In all our time together, I've never been able to jiggle that lock. God knows if I even really tried." She sighed. "You think some things will never change… and then they do. Everything can change."

Even an hour after Samantha left, and Dex was at the airport waiting for his sister, he couldn't shake her words. She'd said his heart was locked, but he'd always thought that it was stone-cold and dead—just like his chances of a reconciliation with his parents. What he'd accepted was a lie, though.

His heart was alive and open to the hurt of Danica's deception. Why did it hurt, though? She was just a woman. Dozens had played him before. Why should she be different?

You became different when you fell in love with her, Harper.

Another unwanted thought.

As much as he didn't want his sister in Las Vegas, Dex was relieved that she appeared in his sights in time to disperse the realization that he was in love with the woman who'd taken away his career.

"I can get a taxi and go straight to a hotel and talk to Danica Blue tomorrow," Erin said flatly, muscling a duffel bag and an equally bulky purse to where he stood semi-disguised in a ball cap and sunglasses. "Or I can hug my brother."

"Get over here, you damn pest."

Erin hurled herself at him, squeezing tight the way she had the few times he'd come home. "Are you all right? All I know is what the news tells."

"It's you I'm worried about."

"Don't be. I'm tougher than you think." She eased away, swiping his hat and putting it on herself backward. It emphasized the dark makeup lining her blue eyes. "I *am* hungry, though."

Dex bought her a soft pretzel and a Coke, then they sat down at a quiet table away from the bustle of passengers.

"You need to go home, Erin."

"I'll do that," she said carefully, "but not before I hear what Danica has to say about this documentary thing. And not before I tell you…that I'm leaving Oregon."

"What? The farm's paid for. It's where you grew up."

"I'm signing it over to you, since you're the one who paid for it. You can sell it and keep the money. Every time I turn around there's a story about a celebrity selling off his assets because Vegas is too costly. In case you don't get back on your feet—"

"I'm far from broke," he told her, unable to kill the smile that tipped up a corner of his mouth. Her concern humbled him. "Maybe tabloids reported that I spent my paychecks as soon as I got them, but I didn't. The farm was a gift. Yours to keep."

"A gift that's forcing me to stay in Gunner. I didn't build things with Dad and Grandpa. That was you. I'm not interested in keeping the land in the family. Again, you."

"The only thing worse than being on the outs with Dad when he died, and not being able to come home for Mom's funeral, would be if something happened to you, Erin."

"Bad things can happen in Gunner."

"You're safer at home, not with me in this city."

"I think Las Vegas and you are incredible," she said. "But I outgrew following you around. I'm moving to California. There's a career waiting for me. Williams-Sonoma."

"What about your videos?"

"I can do both. There's just the farm to deal with."

"Mom and Dad wouldn't agree with you running off to California."

"It's not their choice. It's mine. Be in my life as my brother, not some faraway bodyguard. You went against our parents' plans for your life because you wanted to do something different. So do I."

"Mom and Dad—"

"Are gone." Erin put the pretzel aside and gripped his hands. "They're gone. I'm here because I love you as much as they both did. There's no changing my mind about leaving Oregon. There's no stopping me from talking to Danica tomorrow. Okay, Dexter?"

"Erin, I think Danica's out of the equation. I got in her face about contacting you. It wasn't her place."

"When in doubt, damage the relationship." She shook her head, a pitying expression on her oval face.

"There's no relationship. You don't know this woman."

"Google brought me up to speed nicely. She's hot, smart, charitable. Danica's the only woman who cared enough about you to find me. For that, she deserves my time and an apology from you."

"Quartzite. Definitely, take the quartzite." Veda picked up a whitish crystal and pressed it into Danica's palm before sitting at the head of the table in her English Tudor–style dining room. "It'll give you balance and clarity."

The crystals were only part of the loot Veda had acquired from a metaphysical fair during her world-tour honeymoon. Experiencing romance across the globe with the love of her life suited her well. Vivacious smile. Glowing almond-brown complexion. Peaceful aura.

Danica wanted to leap off her seat at the foot of the table and wiggle in closer to where her best friend sat. Maybe some of that happiness would rub off on her. But Danica knew it was hard-won, and she wasn't quite sure she had the fight in her.

Veda laced her fingers beneath her chin. Her ring shot spears of light off the room's chandelier. The bling was designed specifically for her, a wedding-day gift from her husband. So was the house—no, *manor,* as Willa Smart had bragged only a thousand times when she showed Danica the article from the *Las Vegas Sun. Forbes-list jewelry designer snags Las Vegas's hottest historical property.* "Danica, there's only so much a crystal can accomplish against negative energy. My mom's company has a new online compatibility test. It's *the* most advanced of its kind."

"This girl—" Danica pointed her thumbs at herself "—is not going to be a guinea pig for Dating Done Smart."

"Aren't you having relationship problems?"

"I'm not in a relationship."

"Sad face." Veda drew a finger down her cheek. "Those condoms in your bachelorette-party bag have an expiration date, and you won't even get to use them."

I wouldn't say that. Danica renewed her interest in her margarita.

"Is there something…I don't know…unresolved going on with Marion?"

Danica choked on the drink. "Nope, nada, zilch, zero—"

"Got it. I've been gone only a few weeks, but I'm completely out of the loop. Mom and Cap told me what your folks tried to pull. The part that blows my mind is that *Marion Reeves* let them guilt-trip him. Goes to show the Blues can really put on the pressure."

"You sound worried."

"I'm not." Veda giggled, but her raised eyebrows said, *Should I be?*

Danica supposed she couldn't fault her friend for harboring concern. Tem could throw a vicious tantrum, and former bodybuilder Marshall had an innate "Fear me" vibe going. Though dispelled, the accusation that he'd threatened the former owner into selling the Las Vegas Slayers to him only underscored that.

"When it comes to my family, you are loved all around, V."

Veda perked up at that. "Have another crystal. The candids from the wedding are in, FYI."

She moved the drinks to one side of the table and set up her laptop in front of Danica so they could browse the photos. "This one is my favorite of you. Mom said it's heartbreaking." She enlarged a shot of Danica and the two flower girls. In full bridesmaid's gown and makeup, she was parked on the bridal suite's floor, comforting the girl who'd puked up rose petals, while the other girl—who'd earlier kicked her ankle in a hissy fit—cuddled up to her.

"Good lighting. Exquisite gowns. Cute kids." Danica smiled but felt the beginnings of an itch behind her eyes.

"No, it's the story," her friend insisted. "Completely beautiful. You look so maternal. That's why Mom finds it heartbreaking. You wanted kids of your own, but it didn't happen."

"Let's see the rest." Danica was already minimizing the image.

Veda fell silent for a long moment. "There is this one—" she maneuvered her finger over the track pad "—that Cap found interesting."

Danica was surprised by that. Veda's war-vet father was the type to glance at a photo, then pass it off to someone else without a single comment.

Filling the screen was a photograph that strapped Danica to her seat. She and Dex holding hands beneath the Mandarin Oriental's ceiling of bubbles.

"Um." Veda gently closed the laptop. "I'm going to

have to take this away now. You're getting tears all over my keyboard, m'kay?"

Danica bawled, and in her well-meaning way, Veda wheedled the details out of her. Veda had been relieved that the high-end, easy-tear-wrapper condoms hadn't been doomed to expire, and she'd been empathetic about Danica and Dex's argument. Only a day had passed since the fight in her office, yet Danica felt as if she'd been missing him for years.

When Veda swiped Danica's phone to make a call, Danica got herself together. The Ball Buster didn't cry, certainly not over a man who couldn't peer past his own defenses to see a woman who frankly—and probably unwisely—cared for him.

Migrating to the living room, the women played nickel-and-dime poker on the floor, chatting about anything but men. That is, until Mekhi Corrine strode in, fresh from a workout in athletic wear with his dark-chocolate skin and his jet-black hair, shaved at the sides of his head, glistening with perspiration. "Y'all. There is a *tight* Corvette in our driveway."

"Corvette?" Danica sprang up, her gaze shooting accusingly to her friend.

Veda gathered all the poker change and pranced to her husband with a guilty-as-sin expression.

Mekhi banded his arms around Veda from behind. Their voices followed Danica as she dashed for the foyer.

"What's wrong with her?"

"She's in love."

Danica didn't slow her stride until she'd reached the winding, rosebush-lined driveway. There was Dex behind the wheel of his superhero sports car. "Veda interfered," she began. "I had no knowledge—"

"Yeah?" Dex watched her behind a pair of midnight-black sunglasses. "And how does it make you feel to be on the receiving end of that?"

"Can we do this without the psychology stuff?"

"Do what?"

"Apologize."

Dex leaned out the window, muscles flexing as he reached for her.

Kneeling, she rested against the car door with her hands curling into the collar of his hunter-green shirt and his arms gripping her. "I'm sorry," she whispered repeatedly.

"God, Danica. *I'm* sorry." He swallowed her apologies in a crushing kiss. "This is all I want. You're all I want."

Me, too.

If only Danica could let herself say the words.

Chapter 13

The mile marker for *reckless* was a dot in the rearview mirror. If sleeping together in secret didn't push them past reckless, and getting so close to each other that a fight could turn them inside out didn't, either, then beyond a doubt hitting up popular paparazzi haunt Joel Robuchon to share the sixteen-course tasting menu in the prime of night did.

No name existed for the territory Dex and Danica were in now. *Powerless* was the only explanation he could give to the slam of desire he felt when Danica had appeared in her friend's driveway. After making up with apologies and sex, they'd met his sister for drinks at a casino where Erin had shown off photos of the Harper farmhouse, a timbered area and a forest of cherry fruit trees. Then he'd taken Danica to the Strip for a spur-of-the-moment dinner that had every appearance of a real date.

Until Danica, in that unexplainably shrewd way of hers,

fabricated a story for everyone who stopped to speak en route to their own tables. Curious glances of intrigue turned into looks of disinterest. With a few careful words from Danica, each friend or acquaintance whose eyes glinted with suspicion that the Slayers' former quarterback and the current GM were paired up at Joel Robuchon on a date was manipulated into second-guessing that perception.

When Marshall and Tem entered the restaurant, he was still deciding whether the edginess riding his system was out of concern that they'd get found out, or out of frustration that she couldn't be his.

Danica's back was to the entrance, so Dex leaned forward to murmur, "Want to know what your parents would say if they knew I was wining and dining you?"

"Um, no, actually, I don't. Good news—they don't suspect I'm having frequent filthy sex with you."

"Yeah. Good news."

If she heard the sardonic twinge in his voice, she didn't show it. Under the table her foot roamed up his leg to rest on his crotch. "I'd rather know what you would say if I—"

Damn...hold that thought. "Marshall and Tem are walking this way."

Danica recoiled in time to banish the naughtiness from her expression and greet her parents with an offer to sit at the table. The offer was moot, because Marshall was already gesturing for her to sit beside Dex so that he and his wife could occupy the opposite side of the table.

Then they were facing off again, as they had done at Slayers Club Lounge last month. Except this time Danica was on his side. It made more of a difference than it should. She meant more to him than she should. But it was his own fault that he'd allowed her to unlock his heart.

"Harper, I've been meaning to call you in for a word," Marshall said, folding his hulking frame into the seat his daughter relinquished.

"The league and the feds may be off my ass, but I'm still not passing out names—"

The man's bark of laughter interrupted him. "The future of our ball club is most important to my wife and me. We never planned to wait until the eleventh hour for you to cooperate. Of course, the cooperation would've made things easier on the men we cleared off the team who *didn't* have involvement with the shit storm Al Franco created, but folks say it's better to be safe than sorry. Especially with money and the name Blue on the line."

"Then why a word with him, Pop?" Danica asked. "I cleaned the roster just as you and Ma instructed me to do. Now the trade deadline can come and go, and you can both let Dex move on with his career."

Instinctively, Dex's hand went to her knee. Barely even moving, she draped her hand over his, drawing it up her thigh to the lacy edge of her stocking. Then she just held him there, captured between the soft flesh of her thigh and the strength of her palm.

"Our Danica takes everything seriously. Her clients. The kids at Faith House. You. That's the lawyer in her," Tem said mildly. "Dex, my husband and I simply want to acknowledge that we misjudged your commitment to this game. We know that the next team to sign you up will have made a smart acquisition."

That Mona Lisa smirk created a kaleidoscope of unspoken messages that Dex didn't want to deal with now. There was already speculation that his name had come up in connection with a few *possibly interested* teams, but as his agent, Shaw, was always quick to remind him, an unsigned deal wasn't a deal at all.

"I appreciate that," Dex replied. "Whatever good comes next is a debt I'll owe to Danica. People don't see how damn fortunate they are to have her on their side. I was one of them. But she showed me who she really is, who I really am."

Her sidelong glance was awash in joy.

"Danica has many friends." Tem twisted around the half-empty bottle of wine to read the label. "Marshall and I would stay and give a toast to her dedication to these… projects…that she takes on. But we have a business dinner. In fact, Danica, join us."

"Can't, Ma. I have a few things to finish up with Dex."

"Then I will call you later. Answer the phone, Danica." Tem twirled off her chair, and her husband followed her deeper into the ritzy dining room.

"There's something frosty about Tem tonight," Dex said to Danica.

"Tem *is* frosty. She and Pop think I'm an easy study. An open book."

"That's what you've been letting them think."

"Always seemed easier that way, the best way to get what I want. Adapting to what *they* want me to do or say or be. Guess manipulation's been my crutch for so long that I can't make a clean break."

"You don't manipulate when you're caught off guard, Danica."

"Shh," she whispered playfully. "That's our secret."

You mean I'm your secret. Because you're the one with everything left to lose.

For that reason, for her, he was willing to play the role she'd given him, while he waited for another NFL franchise in another city to give him a reason to let her go.

* * *

"Dex Harper's changed. He's not his usual angry self with reporters and paparazzi. What did you do to make him cooperate with the press?"

Danica glanced at her phone, puzzled at the first words out of her mother's mouth after the heavy question *"Are you alone?"*

Without exactly lying, Danica had confirmed she was alone—at that moment Dex was in his living room and she was resting against the console table that was in the next room.

She, naturally, didn't add that she was in a gorgeous house on a thickly wooded lot that offered the most authentic interpretation of autumn she'd ever happened upon in Las Vegas. Or that the property belonged to last season's hottest NFL quarterback, and she was a solid five minutes away from letting him unzip her dress and inhibitions.

Tem's next question made her wish that she'd powered off the phone or left it in her Boxster so she wouldn't have to think about it. But Tem had sounded strangely somber when she'd said to Danica in the restaurant, "Answer the phone."

"To go from lawless to a charmer in only weeks is a complete one-eighty. I'll ask again. What did you do to make Dex Harper start cooperating with the press?"

Oh, just bartered my heart. Whatever it takes, right? If only it were as simple as that. "Convinced him."

"Your father and I have sources that tell us his tide's about to turn. Your…efforts…are about to pay off."

"That's what I was hoping for."

"Is it, Danica?"

Tem mercifully didn't dawdle on the line for a reaction. She hung up, and Danica flipped the phone over and over in her hands.

Was this what she'd been hoping for? She and Dex had come together to get him onto another NFL team this season. If it happened, the easiest thing to do would be to let him go.

After all, he didn't know that she'd broken her most important rule by falling in love with him. She'd never said the words, and likely never would. It was too big of a chance to take. Perhaps he didn't feel the same way, and she'd pegged him wrong the way she had Marion. Maybe he'd decide she was too challenging to keep in his life, the way Ollie had after only a few dates.

What if Dex had healed her heart only to break it all over again?

Was he too unpredictable to trust?

"Dex," she said, setting aside the phone and retrieving his chessboard from a nearby table. "Up to taking me on?"

He rose from the sofa to effortlessly cart the coffee table out of the way. "Who told you I was a chess player?"

"Your Slayers file. It's listed as a hobby." Danica set up the game on the floor, observing the play of muscle on his form as he sank down across from her on the high-twisted rug.

"Why do I feel like this is going to decide something, Danica?"

Because it is. I don't know any other way to trust what I'm feeling.

They played, each move more strategic than the last. And in what seemed simultaneously like a blink and a thousand years, Danica found herself stuck with nowhere to move her rook without inviting defeat. "You beat me."

"The victory's not official until I say checkmate."

"Dex, it's done. You outmatched me."

Danica made her final move, and he whispered, "Check-mate."

She stuck out her hand for a sportsmanlike shake.

"What was on the line with that game, Danica?"

"Us." She got to her feet. "I can't predict you, so it wouldn't be smart to trust—"

Dex was in front of her before she could grab her purse from where she'd dropped it on the sofa. His size, his strength, the soul that was revealed in his blazing eyes, stole her breath. "A damn chess game doesn't factor into us. I defeated you, but I can't predict what you'll do, Danica. Sometimes it's not all about knowing what's going to happen next. It's about believing. In words. Or a touch. Or your instincts."

"My instincts have been wrong before."

"Then believe what I say. Believe what you feel when I touch you, Danica." Dex raised her hands to his mouth, and watching her face, he pressed a slow, openmouthed kiss on her palm. "Quit running. Playing games and setting rules can't protect you."

Danica pulled back her hands and went for her purse. But she didn't throw the strap over her shoulder and walk out. She reached in and drew out the pink-cellophane-wrapped pair of sex dice—the last of the party favors from her friend's bachelorette party.

They'd used the entire travel-sized bottle of massage oil during "I'm sorry" sex earlier. "The plan was to use everything in the bag," she said. "This is all that's left."

Dex unwrapped the dice and rolled each die to see the possibilities. "What I want to do isn't on these dice. And we don't need more games...."

He reached for her, and they tumbled onto the floor. Their wild embrace came to an abrupt end when she bumped a chess piece with her elbow. He shoved the board off the rug, and the pieces hit the hardwood with a round of clacking sounds.

If this was the end of the road, she wanted to take him greedily, enjoy him selfishly.

With her breath shallow, Danica stared as he peeled off his clothes, revealing a body as hard and precisely cut as stone. She'd loved his body even before she had fantasized about being bold enough to touch him.

She reached for his hands, bringing him back down onto the floor. Hovering over him, she took inventory with her lips, kissing his biceps, his pecs, his abs, his pelvic bones. Lightly she ran her nails over the curling hair at his crotch, and then she welcomed him into her mouth. Each moment brought him deeper; each moan made her wetter. The memory of his taste and how his flesh responded to her touch was what she wanted to take away.

So she took. Refusing to be denied when he tried to slip from her mouth, she gave him a meaningful look, and with tongue and heat and teeth and lips, she pulled from him rapture that had him fisting her hair, groaning roughly and rocking her entire being with his trembles.

"*Damn. Damn,* you're killing me, Danica."

I'm loving you. I love you. I want to trust that you won't hurt me. But she couldn't seem to say those words. She slithered up his sweat-slicked form as he stripped her.

"You're naked…" Turning her onto her back, he stroked his cock, then lifted her leg to nip the tender inside of her thigh. "Now be real with me. I deserve that."

It was no secret that she cared about him as a friend. She knew that he appreciated her, trusted her and was addicted to the passion they brought out in each other.

But to tell him she loved him would be a mistake, wouldn't it?

"No talking. Just touching," she said.

"Is that a rule?"

"For tonight, yeah, it is."

Relenting with a clipped incline of his head, as if to say, *As you wish, then,* he spread her thighs, her folds, and then he suckled her flesh into his mouth.

Danica's ears rang under the attack of her own cries. She couldn't twist away from the intensity, couldn't hide from the thrash of lust and love. She bowed up to watch, only to throw her head back as the first orgasm vibrated through her. The next he lured from her with a single deep thrust.

She was so sensitive to him, so far gone already...and yet he wanted more.

Pulling her to her feet, he stared into her face. "I'm going to break that rule, Danica." He bent to kiss her forehead, even though sweat caused her wispy bangs to stick to her skin. "I love you. Now I know what it's like to say that—to even have a reason to."

"Dex..."

"It doesn't have to change our lives."

Except it freaking *absolutely* did. Because Danica knew physically, emotionally, spiritually and every other possible way that it was true. He'd never lied to her.

His mouth met hers. "You said you didn't know if I liked you. I'm going to take the guess out of that. I do like you."

Danica grinned. "I like you, too."

"Oh, yeah?"

"Yeah." She turned slowly to face the side of the sofa. Gripping the sofa's arm, she pushed her booty to his crotch. Gyrating her hips, she bounced against him. She felt his teeth grazing her shoulder blade, and then his hands were on her hips.

"Danica, are you sure this is what you want?"

"I'm sure."

"I won't hurt you," he promised from behind her.

"I believe you, Dex." And as he came to her, holding

her and kissing her and gently taking what she offered, she gave him something she'd given no other man: herself, completely.

Of his own volition, Marion checked up on Danica. Getting in her face was one way to do it, but that had proven to be a failing approach. So he would tap another source for the information he wanted.

He swaggered into the visitors' wing of the Silver Hills Estates senior-living compound, smoothing a hand over his Armani necktie as he scanned the Wall of Friends photo collection in the lobby.

The woman he waited for was smiling brilliantly back at him from a photograph. People called her type *quirky,* but to a man whose family made its own luck and whose see-it-to-believe-it mentality had paved the way for all his successes, she was *weird.*

Not to say he didn't have love for her. In spite of her eccentricities, she was trustworthy. That trustworthiness was what comforted him. She had what he wanted.

The nameplate beneath it had been updated: Veda Smart-Corrine.

He gave a cursory look at the rest of the images, tensing when he saw Danica's photo under the Benefactor Buddies section. She had a crinkly-eyed smile with a little-bit-naughty edge to her mouth. Beauty and sex appeal and sweetness and toughness combined. This photo had been updated, too, he realized. This had been taken after she'd started wearing bangs, after their divorce and even after she'd started to change.

A few days ago she'd invited him to the mansion, the place that held all of their history, and had offered to give him the keys to the house.

Offered because he'd refused to take the keys or listen

to her crazy talk about the place being haunted. Not with that woo-woo negative-energy shit her friend believed in, but memories. A legal split wasn't enough, and she wanted to give him back what she'd claimed had never belonged to her.

Marion had to know if getting rid of the house was just Danica's angry reaction to the crap he'd let her parents drag him into.

About ten minutes after the Silver Hills Estates receptionist paged her, Veda strolled into the lobby and escorted him to a main-floor office that looked as though all it was missing was a crystal ball and a cashbox.

"Did you and Mekhi get the wedding gift I sent?" he said, kissing her cheek, not directly saying he didn't appreciate being slighted out of an invitation to the event.

"We did. Thanks. Platinum dinnerware is really generous, Marion." Veda went to a fancy cage in the corner of the room and extracted a white rabbit with a gray front paw.

At his puzzled frown, she kissed the rabbit's twitching nose. "This is Moon. I found her not too long ago, and couldn't let her go. Spending time with her is rather comforting to our residents. Fate at work, huh?"

Marion only continued to frown.

"About the dinnerware," she said after a span of silence. "I don't know if we should keep an extravagant gift like that."

"Keep it. It doesn't seem right that when people get divorced they have to divide their friends like assets."

"I'm Danica's closest friend, so I know that you were doing other women behind her back." Veda shrugged, cuddling the damn rabbit as she sat at her desk. "Plus, I've always had the impression that you only tolerate me."

"Danica tried to give me the keys to the house. She

said it's 'haunted.' What have you been filling her head with, Veda?"

"Notions that she should be happy. She hasn't been happy living in that house. Marion, she's moving on, that's all."

"Moving on?" Marion eased a hip onto the corner of her desk. "To what?"

"To the life *she* wants to live." She held the rabbit with one hand and patted his thigh with the other. "We can't all change and expect her to stay the same. She's finding out who she is and who she wants to be with. Right under our noses, Danica fell in love with someone who's a better man because he let her into his life."

Marion searched her face. "Damn…that quarterback. Dex Harper."

"Don't get in the way. It's okay to let her go now, Marion. It's okay for you to take your life off pause, too. That's why you're here—to find validation." Veda got up, rifled through a bowl of crystals and held one toward him. "Rhodonite, for forgiveness and banishing fear. It'll give you the courage to let Danica and yourself move on."

"I don't go for that woo-woo stuff, Veda. As for courage, I already have it."

Veda smiled, satisfied. "Then what are you still doing here?"

Chapter 14

Marshall and Tem didn't call an eight-o'clock meeting unless there was an urgent development that required a quick decision that affected the franchise.

Pumped with adrenaline, Danica marched in her business suit and bustier blouse to the operations staff conference room. A secretary opened the doors for her, unveiling the long mahogany table, tall chairs and an oversized replica of the Las Vegas Slayers logo that glowed beneath track lighting.

Colleagues toting thermoses, Starbucks cups, pastries and electronic tablets meandered about. Lilith, settled in next to the administration coordinator, Antoine Isaiah, waved Danica over to the vacant seat beside her. In front of her were the remnants of some sort of flaky pastry and an empty to-go cup that still held the aroma of a vanilla latte.

In fact, crumpled napkins, crumbs and half-drunk beverages could be found all around the table.

Danica checked her wristwatch. Eight sharp. "How early did everyone get here?"

Lilith quirked an eyebrow. "We all got here on time. Seven-thirty."

Whipping out her smartphone, Danica confirmed that Tem's text message had instructed her to be present at eight for the meeting—not seven-thirty. Why mislead the general manager to arrive a half hour late for what must have been an important discussion?

"If there are no questions, y'all are free to leave," Marshall announced.

Danica's head snapped up. *She'd missed the meeting!* It wasn't savvy for the GM to ever appear out of the loop. "I have a question, sir. What the hell just happened?"

"We have further details for the GM and HC," Marshall addressed the room. With a flick of his wrist, he dismissed the others.

Amazed, Danica watched them go. She stopped Lilith with a tap on her arm. Even her assistant had been given the correct start time. "What did I just walk in on?"

Lilith's glance of sympathy was strange. "Boss, I'm sorry. Offense change. Brock Corday's out as starting QB."

To avoid repeating *what* again, Danica pressed her freshly glossed lips together. She and Kip Claussen remained seated as waitstaff cleaned the tabletop and set out fresh pitchers of water and coffee. A server rolled a cart of pastries to them. Kip grabbed a bear claw, and Danica took two.

"Danica, you look out of sorts." Tem, in her warm-toned designer ensemble, looked, of course, the exact opposite of "out of sorts."

"You gave me the wrong meeting time. Why didn't anyone call me?"

"Your assistant, Lilith, took detailed notes. I asked her to be especially diligent. Marshall?"

"Brock Corday's not healthy enough for us to pin the rest of the season on him. We're making an offer to Dex Harper. I want him and his agent here today. Lilith's arranging the appointment now." Marshall turned toward Kip. "If Harper's ready to work—and I think he will be—I want you to start him on passes this afternoon. Good?"

"Good."

No, not good! Bad. Unbelievable. "Dex is finished with this team. That was made abundantly clear. *You* gave the order to release him and bring someone else on."

"Things change. Adapting is key. Corday's injury makes him too unpredictable. He's also too safe outside the pocket, too slow of a reader. This team needs a risk-taker. Dex's rookie team has been making noise about courting him, but we're prepared to act. Our offer will get Dex Harper back where he belongs—on this team."

And out of Danica's life in every way but what would be a strictly employer-employee relationship....

"I told you to always be sensible," Tem said softly, focusing her gaze on anything but her daughter.

Marshall excused Kip, and when the coach had left, Marshall turned to her. "Confidentially, we'll need a statement from both you and Harper, Danica. The personal relationship ends before he signs any papers for our franchise."

"Wait—"

"Don't insult us by denying that you're involved with him," Tem said. "You were very clever to hide your relationship with him in plain sight."

"I wasn't going to deny it. If bringing Dex to this team is a ploy to stop me from being with him, to turn me back around to Marion, it won't work. Marion's with someone else now. *I'm* with someone else."

"You're not 'with' Dex Harper. That's ridiculous. Know what kind of trouble you'd be asking for?"

"What's so wrong with Dex and me being together? Is it because he's white and I'm black?"

"Of course not. You know we don't care about that. We care about *you.*"

"And I care about Dex."

"Here's what's wrong with you being with that man. The GM cannot have a sexual relationship with an employee—let alone the damn quarterback!" Marshall went for the breast pocket of his jacket. Antacids. She'd really done it now.

Shame churned inside Danica. Was this what Charlotte experienced when she and Nate had been found out? Was this what Martha dealt with on a weekly basis, living under their parents' roof?

"I love him."

Tem stamped her foot. "I cannot imagine *you* would fall into this trap. Does he know you love him?"

Love wasn't a trap, though. Finally, Danica could see that. "I didn't tell him."

"Nor will you. Think of how it would look if the public knew what your so-called friendship was really about. A GM protects the interests of the *team,* not her sex drive." Tem sighed, composing herself. "If you love Dex, don't stand in the way of his career. That man is loyal, driven—just who we need to lead our team."

Just who I need in my life. But Tem was right. Dex's career meant everything to him, and Danica loved him too much to stand in the way.

Dex was certain there was no deeper hell than not getting a spot on a pro roster...until he got one. Sitting in the Slayers' conference room—the same room where he'd been fired—with his agent next to him and the Blues across from him, Dex let the details of the offer register.

He'd be back in his number-eleven uniform, possibly playing next weekend. There would be a formal announcement and press party to show the world that he could shake off being kicked to the curb. And the salary…

Even Shaw, who dealt with seven- and eight-figure deals on a daily basis, had cleared his throat and said, "Excuse me?"

Danica sat stoically in her chair, between her parents, answering questions in a crisp tone of voice that couldn't disguise the hurt hugging her. They both knew that the acquisition would coldly sever their relationship.

Shaw Bordeaux leaned back in his chair. "Makes sense now. Danica, you were grooming him to get him back in as starting QB. That's what this 'cleaning up his reputation' stunt was about from day one."

Dex stared at Danica, who was tapping an ink pen rhythmically against the table. She'd said that firing him had been "just business." Had befriending him, fixing his reputation and sleeping with him also just been business? That would be one effin' shady way to *take one for the team*.

No, he couldn't believe that. She wouldn't give up her body, her heart, for business.

"That's not true," Danica argued. "This franchise's decision-making process is proprietary, but I will tell you that my involvement with Dex—my friendship with him—was not a business strategy for my own or the Slayers' gain."

"If you sign with us, Dex, we'd like you to be looked at by our physicians and back on the practice field as early as today," Tem said. "There's no reason to hold out announcing that the Blue-Eyed Badass is back in Las Vegas."

"Shaw. Marshall and Tem. I need a minute with Danica." Dex rose from his chair, as did the others.

"We'll give you five. And only five," Marshall said.

When the owners and his agent departed from the room, he walked around to Danica's side of the table. "I'm not going to take this offer."

"What other offer do you have?"

"There isn't another."

"Then don't piss on this opportunity. You love football. You missed your mother's funeral just to take the Slayers through the play-offs. Don't sacrifice your career for me."

In the days following his mother's death, Dex had regretted not realizing what was important. But he was damn glad that the woman in front of him had shown him how to change. "I want to be with you, without all the hiding and pretending. Yeah, I do love football," he told her. "But I love you more, Danica."

"And I love you," she insisted in a broken whisper. "I mean that. I love you *so* much. That's why I'm telling you this one final time. Take the offer."

Suddenly the owners crowded back into the conference room, followed by Shaw.

Danica's agitated glance at her father was met with a cold "We gave you your five minutes. Back to business."

A waiter ushered in a bottle of Cristal and a tray of flutes. Danica politely accepted a flute and put as much space between herself and the others as she could without exiting the room.

"I didn't officially decide anything," Dex reminded the group in a growl.

"A toast to…wise decisions," Tem Blue suggested, walking over to Danica and raising her glass to her daughter's. "To being sensible. To the hope that Number Eleven starts next Sunday."

* * *

"No one should be depressed on a Friday night."

Making room for Martha, Danica folded her legs beneath her on the cushiony wicker sofa. They were on the "patio" that seemed more like an outdoor living room with its stone columns, ceiling fans, striking fireplace and all-weather television. The space, designed for entertainment and envy, was nothing short of what she expected her parents to own.

The housewarming party was an extravagant event. Guests filling up on liquor and barbecue were everywhere—poolside, in the gardens, inside the house on all three floors. Vehicles practically blocked street access, but Danica would worry about that later, once she figured out a way to escape the luxurious cage that was her parents' home.

And Martha's. It was easy to forget that this was also her residence. Probably because she still hadn't moved her things out of the Bellagio. Marshall and Tem had grown impatient with her and stated that Martha would be responsible for the Bellagio villa's rental payments unless she cleared out.

"Who says I'm depressed?" Danica challenged over the cacophony of sports TV, blaring music and conversation.

"Mike's Hard Lemonade. That's your third. Plus, you downed the piña colada I fixed you when you got here. You've got me out-boozed." Her sister scoped out their surroundings, then hopped off the sofa. Her girlish, glittery crochet sweater fell past her underpants-short shorts. "Shake off the edge. C'mon."

Danica followed her to the guests swaying and shaking it by the pool.

"Danni, you've seemed sort of unhappy these past few days."

"Just a lot of changes to digest."

"Def. That TMZ report about Marion seen 'canoodling' with that singer he's working with now. You were obviously relieved about that one, though. Pretty admirable of you to wish him well." Martha shifted her weight from one high heel to the other. "Then there's the team. Brock Corday's out and Dex Harper's in. I wonder how he'll do out-of-town on Sunday."

"Pop, Ma and Kip are optimistic. As am I." Danica gave her drink a frown. Even she could hear the note of wistfulness. Maybe it was time for caffeine if she didn't have the energy to keep the reins tight on her emotions.

"Could you be any less enthusiastic? I thought you'd be jazzed about having man candy like that at such easy access."

"Except it's a no-access situation, since he's our quarterback and I'm the GM."

The regret in Danica's voice couldn't be masked, and the enormity of it hung between the two sisters.

"I was right, then," Martha muttered. "I can tell when two people are on fire for each other, and the two of you had lust written all over you when he came to your office that day."

"Who did you tell?"

"No one," her sister insisted, looking offended. "I tried to convince myself I was wrong, because you'd never risk upsetting Ma and Pop. So it seems *that* was the thing I was wrong about."

"They know. They're not pleased with me."

"Welcome to the We Pissed Off Our Parents Sisterhood," Martha said dryly.

Danica contemplated her drink.

"Too soon for jokes?"

"What's funny about losing their high opinion of me *and* losing Dex?"

Martha shrugged. "Can't think of anything, put on the spot like this, but give me some time—"

"Enough. Please."

Martha let up, for a good three seconds. "Let's jump," she proposed.

Danica's brain tripped over the final scenes of *Thelma and Louise*. "Jump *where?*"

"In the water." Martha circled a finger at the well-lit pool. "It's a crazy idea. Just do it."

What would it feel like to get an idea and just act on it, without analyzing and finding reasons to play it safe? Danica stared at the water. It wasn't double Dutch, but… "I'll jump. But only if you promise me something."

Martha took her hard lemonade and passed it off to a server. "Jeez, what?"

"Take my keys."

"Well, if you're that buzzed, then you shouldn't be diving into a pool."

"No, my house keys, Martha. Marion doesn't want the house. Neither do I. I don't want to live there, and you clearly don't want to live here with Ma and Pop. So please take them, and, please God, fill it with love and babies someday." Danica hooked an arm around her to hug her. "You need to grow up, sis. The house, and the condition that goes with it, might be the push you need."

"A condition? Lay it on me."

"Volunteer at Faith House. It's more than passing out flyers and answering phones, though. Consider it?"

Martha gave her a curious look, but nodded and grabbed Danica's hand. They took off running and jumped into the pool, screaming.

Soaked to the skin and invigorated, Danica resurfaced laughing. She gave Martha a high five. Applause greeted them when they emerged from the pool.

Marshall threatened to close the bar if anyone else got the nerve to take a dip fully clothed. Then he called for a housekeeper to bring out towels.

Patting the terry cloth against her wet shirt and jeans, Danica went into the house to inspect the damage to her makeup. The main-floor powder room was occupied. Upstairs, she tried to recall which doors belonged to what rooms. Linen closet. Bedroom. Makeup room.

Yes, this house included a room devoted to Tem's meticulous beauty routines.

Danica opened the door wider. A little bronzer and mascara wouldn't hurt. She clicked on the lit mirror, then heard murmurs. A man's baritone and a woman's whispered response.

She turned into the hall, peeping into the adjacent room's open doorway. Nate Franco sat at the foot of the bed, with Charlotte pressed beside him. Their hands were locked, their heads bent.

"We could elope."

"Your family wouldn't be cool with that, Lottie."

"Imagine the wedding, though. Your father and my parents would interfere. Danica would exploit it for Slayers publicity—if Ma and Pop don't order her to stop the whole thing." Charlotte zoomed in for a kiss. "I just want to marry you, Nate."

Wounded, Danica dropped back from the doorway. Her older sister was engaged, and yet she wouldn't even share the news with Danica. To her sisters, she was too controlled by the team and their parents to make her own choices.

Danica *did* make a choice—a promise, really—as she moved unseen back downstairs without taking the time to repair her water-ruined makeup and rapidly curling hair. A night's sleep would bring clarity, but she knew she wouldn't break the promise she'd just made to herself.

* * *

After claiming a win in the Midwest, the Slayers traveled back to Las Vegas to prepare for the first home game with Dex Harper back as quarterback. Danica waited with nervous anticipation for the Thursday-afternoon emergency press conference.

Not wanting to distract the team during an away game, Danica had kept her decision a secret. It had almost slipped during last Sunday's second quarter, when their quarterback had been hit hard and trainers rushed the field. There had been no injury, but in the moments that uncertainty polluted the air and Danica had tried to make her way to Dex, her mother had taken her aside.

Remember your duties to this team and this family, Danica. He should be nothing more to you than a man who can win games for us. The team is a machine, and he's just a part of it. There's no place for...love...in our front office.

Now Danica waited in the pressroom, with a mic and a glass of iced water in front of her. She was alone. That morning, when she'd sat down with her parents and said, "I'm resigning from the franchise," she'd hoped they would rationally accept her decision. But Marshall had gotten up in arms and Tem had urged her not to lose sight of what was expected of her.

"I promised myself that I would stop neglecting my heart," she'd told them. "In between getting married and then divorced and taking on this career, I lost myself. I can't be your enforcer in this business anymore. And I'm asking you, as your daughter, to support me when I announce the resignation."

In a very professional—clinical—fashion, her parents had called an emergency meeting and named the administration coordinator as interim general manager while they interviewed in-house and outside candidates. The team *was* a machine, and they'd been able to replace her as easily as one would a defective part.

But she sat alone as the doors opened to the press. Her announcement was met with a flurry of questions. It came as second nature to work her magic and spin the situation to make it appear as if her resignation was an exciting turning point for the team, yet a reporter's simple "What does this development mean for you?" shattered her facade.

Danica looked out over the faces watching her intently. Then she turned, and there were her parents and the head coach standing in the wings. "This means," she said into the mic, "that I'm free to focus on what and who I care about outside of this franchise. I'm president of a nonprofit organization, and spending time with the people who come to Faith House feels right. I'm also in love. Someone said to me that being in love is the best feeling there is, and I think that's true."

The pressroom all but imploded then. Camera flashes and "Who are you in love with?" questions pelted Danica, but she'd said all she would say. As she exited the stage, Kip and her parents shook her hand. At least Marshall and Tem didn't snub her in front of a room filled with media.

Word that an emergency announcement would be made in the pressroom had cleared the practice field. Players and staff crisscrossed the turf, cursing at the interruption, speculating the reason for the press conference, complaining about the brutal physical demands of today's practice. Some headed straight for the building to watch the live broadcast indoors, while others sought the coolers and towels.

An emergency announcement meant something huge was happening, and Dex's instincts were jammed on wary. He went through the motions of toweling off sweat and changing clothes at his locker. The embossed nameplate bearing his name had already been installed. It was one of countless reminders that what he'd pursued for so long was at last his.

But he wasn't free to lay claim to the woman who'd given him back what had been stolen…the woman he loved with a fierceness that was dark, insatiable.

He'd tried to pretend she wasn't ingrained in his soul, that he could face a tomorrow without her in it. Only, his heart defeated the lies, one after the other, and all he could do was want her in silence.

Settling into his place on the team was vicious torture when every day they crossed paths because business either brought her down to his field or him up to the administrative offices. Both worked closely with the head coach, and hadn't a hope in hell of avoiding each other.

He treasured every reason to see her, masochistic bastard that he was. He'd rather be near her this way than to not have her at all. That would do until he could force himself to accept that unlike his NFL career, his relationship with Danica Blue was over.

Unfortunately for him, it was quickly becoming tougher to buy in to that. Today he'd given his all and then some on the practice field, pushing his body beyond its ordinary limits just to keep his mind from chasing Danica.

All that effort disintegrated into grit once he entered the massive team lounge to find her image on every television screen.

Dex nudged one of the offensive coaches. "What's happening? Roster change?"

"The GM's out."

"The hell she is," a woman protested, and Dex and the coach pivoted. Charlotte Blue advanced on them, leaving the team's kicker and the head athletic trainer to venture toward a buffet table without her. She stepped up close, tossing her single sloppy braid over her shoulder. A soft floral scent levitated from her hair. The men had insisted that she was the best-smelling thing on the practice field. "I'd know if my sister was fired."

"Not fired," the coach clarified, pointing with two fingers at the closest television. "Danica quit—resigned. Yo, somebody get the volume up on this TV."

Charlotte's mouth dropped open, but she didn't speak— just mutely turned forward and watched through the forest of tall bodies loitering in front of the screen.

Danica sat in front of a mic without a single person beside her. Bursts of camera lights shone on her beautiful face, which he could visualize in his dreams with exact accuracy.

"Unreal," muttered Charlotte, who'd found her voice again. "Danica wouldn't in a million lifetimes walk away from this team."

"Snap out of your denial, Charlotte," the coach suggested. "It's already happened, and they've named the interim GM."

"Damn," someone hollered. "New GM now? Hey, Coach Claussen, are you planning on rolling out, too?"

"No," Kip retorted, "I'll still be here to put you through drills until I see perfection."

"Coach Claussen," Charlotte said over the din as the man was striding toward the exit, "did you know about this?"

"No. Pressroom's my next stop. Coming?"

Charlotte paused just as Danica said into her mic, "I'm also in love."

Dex froze, slinging his gaze from Charlotte and Kip to the television. Reporters were yelling over each other, all demanding the same information. A name.

Who are you in love with?

They all wanted to know.

And Dex wanted her to tell them. *Say it, Danica. Tell them you're in love with me. Tell them I'm your man.*

But she shut them down, speaking nothing more on the matter—as though she hadn't just resigned and confessed to being in love in one quick slice.

"I'll go later," Charlotte told Kip, but her stare had stalled on Dex in a way that made him feel guilty and affronted at the same time.

When he'd found an opportunity to exit the lounge without calling attention to himself, he wasn't surprised that Charlotte showed up on his trail.

"What've you got going on with Danica?" It was a softly spoken demand, yet tension was all but written on her, from the jiggle of one of her feet to the way she'd crossed her arms and was gripping her waist.

"Ask Danica."

"She announced to the nation that she's resigning from the Slayers. She followed that up with the confession that she's in love. If Danica had wanted to tell me what's going on, she would've." Charlotte unwound her arms, and there was a flare of temper in her eyes. "So I'm asking you. Are you the man she's in love with?"

"I'm not going to speak for her. But I'll tell you this. I love Danica."

"Really. You love the woman who fired you?"

"Yeah. Why's that difficult to accept? You love Nate Franco in spite of what he and his family did to you."

Charlotte sighed. "Fair enough. Just let me say something. Last summer, when you and I needed an ally, we helped each other out. But none of that will matter if you hurt my sister."

"Fair enough," he said stoically, echoing her words.

Once she started walking in the direction from which she'd come, Dex took off for the administration complex.

He arrived on the ninth floor to find Danica's office door shut and her assistant's open. He rapped on the door a few times, and Lilith greeted him with a sweet smile. "Danica hasn't come back up here yet, but I'm expecting her to any minute."

"I can wait out here."

"Better idea," she countered, scurrying around her desk, across the corridor and to Danica's office. The door was unlocked and she gestured for him to enter. "Wait in here. Tell Danica that I'm taking a late lunch at the Medici Café. Don't forget."

Dex sat in the same striped chair he'd claimed when he first joined Danica in this space that night in September. A solid five minutes had passed before the door opened and Danica stepped inside wearing a dress the color of eggplant. The thing shimmied when she moved, and was already playing his control like a fiddle.

"Dex."

"You're not surprised to see me."

"I passed Lily in the hall. She said she'd asked you to wait in here."

"Then she also told you about the Medici Café?"

She shook her head. "What about it?"

"'Tell Danica I'm taking a late lunch at the Medici Café. Don't forget,'" he quoted.

"That place is at the Ritz…in Henderson. It's a twenty-minute one-way drive in decent traffic. She made herself scarce."

"Then add her to the list of people who know about us. Add Charlotte, too. She all but cornered me, and warned me not to hurt you."

"Sorry. My sisters and I are long overdue for a heart-to-heart." Danica locked the door, then crossed the room to him, letting her hands fall to his shoulders. "I'm going to miss seeing you here like this, Dex."

"Why did you make that announcement? Why are you giving up this career, Danica?" He took her hands, kissing the backs of each one. "Working for this franchise, working with your family, is important to you."

"That was before you and I changed. Before love got to us."

"You wouldn't give the press my name."

"It wasn't the right time."

"When will it be, Danica? See where this puts us? This morning all I had to confront was the fact that I'm not free to be with you in private, for the sake of your career and mine. But at least we could still see each other here, as colleagues. Now that you've resigned and still want us to be a secret, I lose even that."

Danica withdrew her hands from his. "You're still adjusting to this roster and don't need the distraction of a scandal. There's the game on Sunday to think about."

"Screw the game. That's not more important than your happiness and how damn happy you make me." Dex rested his elbows on his thighs, looking up at her. "I don't want to ease the public into the idea of you and me together. I want to think about how grateful I am that you're my woman."

"Dex…" Danica angled closer, reaching to tunnel her fingers into his hair.

He closed his eyes, savoring her light touch.

"Dex."

Her voice was close now, her breath teasing his jaw. Turning toward her, he took her mouth with his. God, it had been too long since he'd tasted her, since he'd felt her tongue curl so, so slowly around his.

"Hey," she said, and he opened his eyes. "Sit back. Your woman wants you to make some room for her."

He let her perch on his lap with her back against his chest, and being with her like this—body to body—was the only thing he knew with his entire existence was right. "What's the future look like to you, Danica?"

He felt her contemplative sigh against his chest, and she said, "The future looks like truth. No secrets. Just us. And love."

Dex pressed a kiss to her shoulder. "Get up. Your man wants to tell you something."

When she was standing before him, he clasped her hips. The slinky fabric of her dress slid over her skin with ease as he gripped the material and began to pull it upward. Once her thighs were exposed, he leaned forward to dot each one with a kiss. But he kept urging the dress up until he had it bunched beneath her breasts.

Danica's fingers trembled as she gathered the fabric to free his hands. Gently, he scraped his fingertips up her thighs, over the lace triangle of her underwear. He curled a finger around the thin waistband, tugged it taut, then let it snap against her skin.

She moaned, and he grinned. "The future I see looks like home, Danica," he murmured, his lips brushing her belly. "The two of us…a baby. I see myself having that kind of life with you."

"You'd want to be a father?" she whispered.

"To your child. Our child." Dex kissed her abdomen again, cupping her butt, not caring whether this was the right or wrong time to let her know the commitment he could give her that he'd never wanted to offer anyone else. "I want to be the man who can make you feel good for the rest of your life, Danica."

"I'm crying," she whispered, and he glanced up to see

her chocolate-brown eyes sparkle with tears, "because I'm so damn in love with you."

"Want that kind of future with me?" he asked. "Truth, home, love, a baby? We can have all of that, with some crazy-ass adventures thrown in there."

"Crazy-ass adventures was going to be the deal-breaker," she said with a teasing laugh. Then, sobering, she let her bunched dress slide back down her torso and over her hips. "Sunday's going to come before all of that, Dex."

"Danica—"

"This city needs to see you win at home. Get it done." She kissed him deeply. "Our future'll still be there after Sunday."

Dex stood and followed her to the door. Once she unlocked it, he stroked her cheek. "Our future... Don't say it if you don't mean it." Then he opened the door and strode out while he still had the strength to walk away.

Gossip hung over Danica the next few days. But as she stood in a silk spaghetti-strapped dress and a long, knotted pearl necklace, ladling punch from a cauldron beneath a canopy of curling orange and black ribbons at Faith House, she felt at peace. Mostly. She might have publicly walked away from her family's legacy and triggered a national guessing game about just who she was in love with, but she refused to call out the man she loved when he had a game to win.

Tonight, Dex was where he belonged: on the field at Slayers Stadium.

"This is my kind of scene."

Surprised, Danica turned to see her younger sister reaching out for a drink. "A Halloween party for teens?" she said skeptically. "There's no alcohol in that cup, Martha."

"A true partier doesn't require alcohol to have a good time." There was that know-it-all smile that was so distinctively Martha. "I said I'd volunteer. Why not start now?"

"It's Sunday night. You should be at the stadium."

"Danni, *you* should be. It's the fourth quarter and our boys just scored on a turnover. It could go either way. Win or lose, our quarterback would want to see you on the sidelines."

Danica batted away a tangle of ribbons tickling her face. "Martha—"

"Last week, when he was playing, you looked at him on the field like you missed him—like he was a world away. Being in love *is* the best feeling, and I'm glad you feel that way. So go to your man."

She looked around. The party was an uproar of pounding music and noise. Some kids were in costumes, a few were dressed in formal-wear, but most were jeans-and-hoodie clad. Chaperones lurked like ants at a picnic. "I'll be back," Danica said.

Martha snorted, taking away the ladle. "You're going to tell the finest QB in the NFL that you want to be with him—you *won't* be coming back tonight."

No time-outs remained. The Slayers' defense had forced the second turnover of the quarter. Chances were this would be the offense's final possession in the game. In the visitors' territory, Dex would need to send the ball damn near thirty yards to make a scoring play and create a deficit New York wouldn't recover from tonight.

Every second counted; every decision mattered. Pivoting, he escaped the clutch of a linebacker and scanned the field for an open man. His cleats gripped the turf, his heart hammered in his chest, a chorus of thousands of screaming voices battered his ears, but his mind was laser-sharp.

There, a receiver in red and silver. If the man didn't break his speed, he'd be in a prime spot in the end zone to capture the ball by the time Dex passed it downfield. It was a risk that would be regarded as reckless if it didn't work or ingenious if it did.

The safe move would be to grapple for a few yards and take a slide.

Dex released the ball, throwing long...

And connecting.

Hell, yes!

Chaos draped over the stadium, but all Dex saw were teammates slamming into him for hugs and handshakes.

Then, as players, coaches, media and security inundated the field, there was Danica...so feminine and delicate-looking in a thin dress that danced over her glorious curves as she moved with purpose to him.

Dex drew off his helmet, and she ran into his arms, colliding her perfume and pearls with his sweat and mud. Yet she felt as though she was meant to be there.

The atmosphere on the field shifted as speculation hit the onlookers. In his periphery he saw bright flashes and stunned faces, but his focus was on the woman in his arms.

Dex lifted her against him, off her feet, and Danica said with a grin, "Lover, take me away from all this."

"What'd you have in mind?"

"We could get started on that future we talked about...."

"The one with truth and home and love and a baby?"

"Yes. I want all of it, with you."

"What about Thanksgiving in Oregon? I've got this land..."

"Yes."

"What about tonight at my place?"

"Are you trying to see how many times you can get me to say the word *yes*?"

Lit with the fire of love and excitement, he kissed her in the middle of the field. "People will be talking about this all night."

Danica framed his face with her hands. There was strength beneath the softness. "While everyone else is talking the night away, I'm going to be with you…and we'll be *much* too busy to talk."

* * * * *

Don't miss the next book in THE BLUE DYNASTY, *JUST FOR CHRISTMAS NIGHT*
by Lisa Marie Perry.
Martha Blue gets her chance for romance at the most magical time of all—Christmas!
Coming to you December 2014, from
Harlequin Kimani Romance.